Merely Mary Ann by Israel Zangwill

Israel Zangwill was born in London on 21st January 1864, to a family of Jewish immigrants from the Russian Empire.

Zangwill was initially educated in Plymouth and Bristol. At age 9 he was enrolled in the Jews' Free School in Spitalfields in east London. Zangwill excelled here. He began to teach part-time at the school and eventually full time. Whilst teaching he also studied with the University of London and by 1884 had earned his BA with triple honours in philosophy, history, and the sciences.

His writing earned him the sobriquet "the Dickens of the Ghetto" primarily based on his much lauded novel 'Children of the Ghetto: A Study of a Peculiar People' in 1892 and its glimpse of the poverty-stricken life in London's Jewish quarter.

As a writer he was keen to reflect on his political and social outlooks. His simulation of Yiddish sentence structure in English aroused great interest. His mystery work, 'The Big Bow Mystery' (1892) was the first locked room mystery novel.

Zangwill was also involved with narrowly focused Jewish issues as an assimilationist, an early Zionist, and later a territorialist. In the early 1890s he had joined the Lovers of Zion movement in England. In 1897 he joined Theodor Herzl (considered the father of modern political Zionism) in founding the World Zionist Organization.

Zangwill quit the established philosophy of Zionism when his plan for a homeland in Uganda was rejected and founded his own organisation; the Jewish Territorialist Organization. Its stated goal was to create a Jewish homeland in whatever territory in the world could be found for them.

Amongst the challenges in his life he found time to write poetry. He had translated a medieval Jewish poet in 1903 and his volume 'Blind Children' in 1908 shows his promise in this new endeavour.

'The Melting Pot' in 1909 made Zangwill's name as an admired playwright. When the play opened in Washington D.C., former President Theodore Roosevelt leaned over the edge of his box and shouted, "That's a great play, Mr. Zangwill, that's a great play."

Israel Zangwill died on 1st August 1926 in Midhurst, West Sussex.

Index of Contents
MERELY MARY ANN
I
II
III
ISRAEL ZANGWILL – A SHORT BIOGRAPHY
ISRAEL ZANGWILL – A CONCISE BIBLIOGRAPHY

Sometimes Lancelot's bell rang up Mrs. Leadbatter herself, but far more often merely Mary Ann.

The first time Lancelot saw Mary Ann she was cleaning the steps. He avoided treading upon her, being kind to animals. For the moment she was merely a quadruped, whose head was never lifted to the stars. Her faded print dress showed like the quivering hide of some crouching animal. There were strange irregular splashes of pink in the hide, standing out in bright contrast with the neutral background. These were scraps of the original material neatly patched in.

The cold, damp steps gave Lancelot a shudder, for the air was raw. He passed by the prostrate figure as quickly as he could, and hastened to throw himself into the easy-chair before the red fire.

There was a lamp-post before the door, so he knew the house from its neighbours. Baker's Terrace as a whole was a defeated aspiration after gentility. The more auspicious houses were marked by white stones, the steps being scrubbed and hearthstoned almost daily; the gloomier doorsteps were black, except on Sundays. Thus variety was achieved by houses otherwise as monotonous and prosaic as a batch of fourpenny loaves. This was not the reason why the little South London side-street was called Baker's Terrace, though it might well seem so; for Baker was the name of the builder, a worthy gentleman whose years and virtues may still be deciphered on a doddering, round-shouldered stone in a deceased cemetery not far from the scene of his triumphs.

The second time Lancelot saw Mary Ann he did not remember having seen her before. This time she was a biped, and wore a white cap. Besides, he hardly glanced at her. He was in a bad temper, and Beethoven was barking terribly at the intruder who stood quaking in the doorway, so that the crockery clattered on the tea-tray she bore. With a smothered oath Lancelot caught up the fiery little spaniel and rammed him into the pocket of his dressing-gown, where he quivered into silence like a struck gong. While the girl was laying his breakfast, Lancelot, who was looking moodily at the pattern of the carpet as if anxious to improve upon it, was vaguely conscious of relief in being spared his landlady's conversation. For Mrs. Leadbatter was a garrulous body, who suffered from the delusion that small-talk is a form of politeness, and that her conversation was a part of the "all inclusive" her lodgers stipulated for. The disease was hereditary, her father having been a barber, and remarkable for the coolness with which, even as a small boy whose function was lathering and nothing more, he exchanged views about the weather with his victims.

The third time Lancelot saw Mary Ann he noticed that she was rather pretty. She had a slight, well-built figure, not far from tall, small shapely features, and something of a complexion. This did not displease him: she was a little aesthetic touch amid the depressing furniture.

"Don't be afraid, Polly," he said, more kindly. "The little devil won't bite. He's all bark. Call him Beethoven and throw him a bit of sugar."

The girl threw Beethoven the piece of sugar, but did not venture on the name. It seemed to her a long name for such a little dog. As she timidly took the sugar from the basin by the aid of the tongs, Lancelot saw how coarse and red her hand was. It gave him the same sense of repugnance and refrigescence as the cold, damp steps. Something he was about to say froze on his lips. He did not look at Mary Ann for some days; by which time Beethoven had conquered his distrust of her, though she was still distrustful of Beethoven, drawing her skirts tightly about her as if he were a rat. What forced Mary Ann again upon Lancelot's morose consciousness was a glint of winter sunshine that settled on her light brown hair. He said: "By the way, Susan, tell your mistress—or is it your mother?"

Mary Ann shook her head but did not speak.

"Oh: you are not Miss Leadbatter?"

"No; Mary Ann."

She spoke humbly; her eyes were shy and would not meet his. He winced as he heard the name, though her voice was not unmusical.

"Ah, Mary Ann! and I've been calling you Jane all along. Mary Ann what?"

She seemed confused and flushed a little.

"Mary Ann!" she murmured.

"Merely Mary Ann?"

"Yessir."

He smiled. "Seems a sort of white Topsy," he was thinking.

She stood still, holding in her hand the tablecloth she had just folded. Her eyes were downcast, and the glint of sunshine had leapt upon the long lashes.

"Well, Mary Ann, tell your mistress there is a piano coming. It will stand over there—you'll have to move the sideboard somewhere else."

"A piano!" Mary Ann opened her eyes, and Lancelot saw that they were large and pathetic. He could not see the colour for the glint of sunshine that touched them with false fire.

"Yes; I suppose it will have to come up through the window, these staircases are so beastly narrow. Do you never have a stout person in the house, I wonder?"

"Oh yes, sir. We had a lodger here last year as was quite a fat man."

"And did he come up through the window by a pulley?"

He smiled at the image, and expected to see Mary Ann smile in response. He was disappointed when she did not; it was not only that her stolidity made his humour seem feeble—he half wanted to see how she looked when she smiled.

"Oh dear no," said Mary Ann; "he lived on the ground floor!"

"Oh!" murmured Lancelot, feeling the last sparkle taken from his humour. He was damped to the skin by Mary Ann's platitudinarian style of conversation. Despite its prettiness, her face was dulness incarnate.

"Anyhow, remember to take in the piano if I'm out," he said tartly. "I suppose you've seen a piano—you'll know it from a kangaroo?"

"Yessir," breathed Mary Ann.

"Oh, come, that's something. There is some civilisation in Baker's Terrace after all. But are you quite sure?" he went on, the teasing instinct getting the better of him. "Because, you know, you've never seen a kangaroo."

Mary Ann's face lit up a little. "Oh, yes I have, sir; it came to the village fair when I was a girl."

"Oh, indeed!" said Lancelot, a little staggered; "what did it come there for—to buy a new pouch?"

"No, sir; in a circus."

"Ah, in a circus. Then, perhaps, you can play the piano, too."

Mary Ann got very red. "No, sir; missus never showed me how to do that."

Lancelot surrendered himself to a roar of laughter. "This is a real original," he said to himself, just a touch of pity blending with his amusement.

"I suppose, though, you'd be willing to lend a hand occasionally?" he could not resist saying.

"Missus says I must do anything I'm asked," she said, in distress, the tears welling to her eyes. And a merciless bell mercifully sounding from an upper room, she hurried out.

How much Mary Ann did, Lancelot never rightly knew, any more than he knew the number of lodgers in the house, or who cooked his chops in the mysterious regions below stairs. Sometimes he trod on the toes of boots outside doors and vaguely connected them with human beings, peremptory and exacting as himself. To Mary Ann each of those pairs of boots was a personality, with individual hours of rising and retiring, breakfasting and supping, going out and coming in, and special idiosyncrasies of diet and disposition. The population of 5 Baker's Terrace was nine, mostly bell-ringers. Life was one ceaseless round of multifarious duties; with six hours of blessed unconsciousness, if sleep were punctual. All the week long Mary Ann was toiling up and down the stairs or sweeping them, making beds or puddings, polishing boots or fire-irons. Holidays were not in Mary Ann's calendar; and if Sunday ever found her on her knees, it was only when she was scrubbing out the kitchen. All work and no play makes Jack a dull boy; it had not, apparently, made Mary Ann a bright girl.

The piano duly came in through the window like a burglar. It was a good instrument, but hired. Under Lancelot's fingers it sang like a bird and growled like a beast. When the piano was done growling Lancelot usually started. He paced up and down the room, swearing audibly. Then he would sit down at the table and cover ruled paper with hieroglyphics for hours together. His movements were erratic to the verge of mystery. He had no fixed hours for anything; to Mary Ann he was hopeless. At any given moment he might be playing on the piano, or writing on the curiously ruled paper, or stamping about the room, or sitting limp with despair in the one easy-chair, or drinking whisky and water, or smoking a black meerschaum, or reading a book, or lying in bed, or driving away in a hansom, or walking about Heaven alone knew where or why. Even Mrs. Leadbatter, whose experience of life was wider than Mary Ann's, considered his vagaries almost unchristian, though to the highest degree gentlemanly. Sometimes, too, he sported the swallow-tail and the starched breast-plate, which was a wonder to Mary Ann, who knew that waiters were connected only with the most stylish establishments. Baker's Terrace did not wear evening dress.

Mary Ann liked him best in black and white. She thought he looked like the pictures in the young ladies' novelettes, which sometimes caught her eye as she passed newsvendors' shops on errands. Not that she was read in this literature—she had no time for reading. But, even when clothed in rough tweeds, Lancelot had for Mary Ann an aristocratic halo; in his dressing-gown he savoured of the grand Turk. His hands were masterful: the fingers tapering, the nails pedantically polished. He had fair hair, with moustache to match; his brow was high and white, and his grey eyes could flash fire. When he drew himself up to his full height, he threatened the gas globes. Never had No. 5 Baker's Terrace boasted of such a tenant. Altogether, Lancelot loomed large to Mary Ann; she dazzled him with his own boots in humble response, and went about sad after a reprimand for putting his papers in order. Her whole theory of life oscillated in the presence of a being whose views could so run counter to her strongest instincts. And yet, though the universe seemed tumbling about her ears when he told her she must not move a scrap of manuscript, howsoever wildly it lay about the floor or under the bed, she did not for a moment question his sanity. She obeyed him like a dog; uncomprehending, but trustful. But, after all, this was only of a piece with the rest of her life. There was nothing she questioned. Life stood at her bedside every morning in the cold dawn, bearing a day heaped high with duties; and she jumped cheerfully out of her warm bed and took them up one by one, without question or murmur. They were life. Life had no other meaning any more than it has for the omnibus hack, which cannot conceive existence outside shafts, and devoid of the intermittent flick of a whip point. The comparison is somewhat unjust; for Mary Ann did not fare nearly so well as the omnibus hack, having to make her meals off such scraps as even the lodgers sent back. Mrs. Leadbatter was extremely economical, as much so with the provisions in her charge as with those she bought for herself. She sedulously sent up remainders till they were expressly countermanded. Less economical by nature, and hungrier by habit, Mary Ann had much trouble in restraining herself from surreptitious pickings. Her conscience was rarely worsted; still there was a taint of dishonesty in her soul, else had the stairs been less of an ethical battleground for her. Lancelot's advent only made her hungrier; somehow the thought of nibbling at his provisions was too sacrilegious to be entertained. And yet—so queerly are we and life compounded— she was probably less unhappy at this period than Lancelot, who would come home in the vilest of tempers, and tramp the room with thunder on his white brow. Sometimes he and the piano and Beethoven would all be growling together, at other times they would all three be mute; Lancelot crouching in the twilight with his head in his hands; and Beethoven moping in the corner, and the closed piano looming in the background like a coffin of dead music.

One February evening—an evening of sleet and mist—Lancelot, who had gone out in evening dress, returned unexpectedly, bringing with him for the first time a visitor. He was so perturbed that he forgot to use his latchkey, and Mary Ann, who opened the door, heard him say angrily, "Well, I can't slam the door in your face, but I will tell you in your face I don't think it at all gentlemanly of you to force yourself upon me like this."

"My dear Lancelot, when did I ever set up to be a gentleman? You know that was always your part of the contract." And a swarthy, thick-set young man with a big nose lowered the dripping umbrella he had been holding over Lancelot, and stepped from the gloom of the street into the fuscous cheerfulness of the ill-lit passage.

By this time Beethoven, who had been left at home, was in full ebullition upstairs, and darted at the intruder the moment his calves appeared. Beethoven barked with short, sharp snaps, as became a bilious liver-coloured Blenheim spaniel.

"Like master like dog," said the swarthy young man, defending himself at the point of the umbrella. "Really your animal is more intelligent than the overrated common or garden dog, which makes no distinction between people calling in the small hours and people calling in broad daylight under the obvious patronage of its own master. This beast of yours is evidently more in sympathy with its liege lord. Down, Fido, down! I wonder they allow you to keep such noisy creatures—but stay! I was forgetting you keep a piano. After that, I suppose, nothing matters."

Lancelot made no reply, but surprised Beethoven into silence by kicking him out of the way. He lit the gas with a neatly written sheet of music which he rammed into the fire Mary Ann had been keeping up, then as silently he indicated the easy-chair.

"Thank you," said the swarthy young man, taking it. "I would rather see you in it, but as there's only one, I know you wouldn't be feeling a gentleman; and that would make us both uncomfortable."

"'Pon my word, Peter," Lancelot burst forth, "you're enough to provoke a saint."

"'Pon my word, Lancelot," replied Peter imperturbably, "you're more than enough to provoke a sinner. Why, what have you to be ashamed of? You've got one of the cosiest dens in London and one of the comfortablest chairs. Why, it's twice as jolly as the garret we shared at Leipsic—up the ninety stairs."

"We're not in Germany now. I don't want to receive visitors," answered Lancelot sulkily.

"A visitor! you call me a visitor! Lancelot, it's plain you were not telling the truth when you said just now you had forgiven me."

"I had forgiven—and forgotten you."

"Come, that's unkind. It's scarcely three years since I threw up my career as a genius, and you know why I left you, old man. When the first fever of youthful revolt was over, I woke to see things in their true light. I saw how mean it was of me to help to eat up your wretched thousand pounds. Neither of us saw the situation nakedly at first—it was sicklied o'er with Quixotic foolishness. You see, you had the advantage of me. Your governor was a gentleman. He says, 'Very well, if you won't go to Cambridge, if you refuse to enter the Church as the younger son of a blue-blooded but impecunious baronet should, and to step into the living which is fattening for you, then I must refuse to take any further responsibility for your future. Here is a thousand pounds; it is the money I had set aside for your college course. Use it for your musical tomfoolery if you insist, and then—get what living you can.' Which was severe but dignified, unpaternal yet patrician. But what does my governor do? That cantankerous, pig-headed old Philistine—God bless him!—he's got no sense of the respect a father owes to his offspring. Not an atom. You're simply a branch to be run on the lines of the old business, or be shut up altogether. And, by the way, Lancelot, he hasn't altered a jot since those days when—as you remember—the City or starvation was his pleasant alternative. Of course, I preferred starvation—one usually does at nineteen; especially if one knows there's a scion of aristocracy waiting outside to elope with him to Leipsic."

"But you told me you were going back to your dad, because you found you had mistaken your vocation."

"Gospel truth also! My heavens, shall I ever forget the blank horror that grew upon me when I came to understand that music was a science more barbarous than the mathematics that floored me at school, that the life of a musical student, instead of being a delicious whirl of waltz tunes, was 'one dem'd grind,' that seemed to grind out all the soul of the divine art and leave nothing but horrid technicalities about consecutive fifths and suspensions on the dominant? I dare say most people still think of the musician as a being who lives in an enchanted world of sound, rather than as a person greatly occupied with tedious feats of penmanship; just as I myself still think of a prima ballerina not as a hard-working gymnast, but as a fairy, whose existence is all bouquets and lime-light."

"But you had a pretty talent for the piano," said Lancelot in milder accents. "No one forced you to learn composition. You could have learnt anything for the paltry fifteen pounds exacted by the Conservatoire—from the German flute to the grand organ; from singing to scoring band parts."

"No, thank you. Aut Caesar aut nihil. You remember what I always used to say: 'Either Beethoven—' (The spaniel pricked up his ears.) —or bust.' If I could not be a great musician it was hardly worth while enduring the privations of one, especially at another man's expense. So I did the Prodigal Son dodge, as you know, and out of the proceeds sent me your year's exes in that cheque you with your damnable pride sent me back again. And now, old fellow, that I have you face to face at last, can you offer the faintest scintilla of a shadow of a reason for refusing to take that cheque? No, you can't! Nothing but simple beastly stuckuppishness. I saw through you at once; all your heroics were a fraud. I was not your friend, but your protégé—something to practise your chivalry on. You dropped your cloak, and I saw your feet of clay. Well, I tell you straight, I made up my mind at once to be bad friends with you for life; only when I saw your fiery old phiz at Brahmson's I felt a sort of something tugging inside my greatcoat like a thief after my pocket-book, and I kinder knew, as the Americans say, that in half an hour I should be sitting beneath your hospitable roof."

"I beg your pardon—you will have some whisky." He rang the bell violently.

"Don't be a fool—you know I didn't mean that. Well, don't let us quarrel. I have forgiven you for your youthful bounty, and you have forgiven me for chucking it up; and now we are going to drink to the Vaterland," he added, as Mary Ann appeared with a suspicious alacrity.

"Do you know," he went on, when they had taken the first sip of renewed amity dissolved in whisky, "I think I showed more musical soul than you in refusing to trammel my inspiration with the dull rules invented by fools. I suppose you have mastered them all, eh?" He picked up some sheets of manuscript. "Great Scot! How you must have schooled yourself to scribble all this—you, with your restless nature—full scores, too! I hope you don't offer this sort of thing to Brahmson."

"I certainly went there with that intention," admitted Lancelot. "I thought I'd catch Brahmson himself in the evening—he's never in when I call in the morning."

Peter groaned.

"Quixotic as ever! You can't have been long in London then?"

"A year."

"I suppose you'd jump down my throat if I were to ask you how much is left of that—" he hesitated, then turned the sentence facetiously—"of those twenty thousand shillings you were cut off with?"

"Let this vile den answer."

"Don't disparage the den; it's not so bad."

"You are right—I may come to worse. I've been an awful ass. You know how lucky I was while at the Conservatoire—no, you don't. How should you? Well, I carried off some distinctions and a lot of conceit, and came over here thinking Europe would be at my feet in a month. I was only sorry my father died before I could twit him with my triumph. That's candid, isn't it?"

"Yes; you're not such a prig after all," mused Peter; "I saw the old man's death in the paper—your brother Lionel became the bart."

"Yes, poor beggar, I don't hate him half so much as I did. He reminds me of a man invited to dinner which is nothing but flowers and serviettes and silver plate."

"I'd pawn the plate, anyhow," said Peter, with a little laugh.

"He can't touch anything, I tell you; everything's tied up."

"Ah well, he'll get tied up, too. He'll marry an American heiress."

"Confound him! I'd rather see the house extinct first."

"Hoity, toity! She'll be quite as good as any of you."

"I can't discuss this with you, Peter," said Lancelot, gently but firmly. "If there is a word I hate more than the word heiress, it is the word American."

"But why? They're both very good words and better things."

"They both smack of the most vulgar thing in the world—money," said Lancelot, walking hotly about the room. "In America there's no other standard. To make your pile, to strike ile—oh, how I shudder to hear these idioms! And can any one hear the word heiress without immediately thinking of matrimony? Phaugh? It's a prostitution."

"What is? You're not very coherent, my friend."

"Very well, I am incoherent. If a great old family can only bolster up its greatness by alliances with the daughters of oil-strikers, then let the family perish with honour."

"But the daughters of oil-strikers are sometimes very charming creatures. They are polished with their fathers' oil."

"You are right. They reek of it. Pah! I pray to Heaven Lionel will either wed a lady or die a bachelor."

"Yes; but what do you call a lady?" persisted Peter.

Lancelot uttered an impatient snarl, and rang the bell violently. Peter stared in silence. Mary Ann appeared.

"How often am I to tell you to leave my matches on the mantel-shelf?" snapped Lancelot. "You seem to delight to hide them away, as if I had time to play parlour games with you."

Mary Ann silently went to the mantel-piece, handed him the matches, and left the room without a word.

"I, say, Lancelot, adversity doesn't seem to have agreed with you," said Peter severely. "That poor girl's eyes were quite wet when she went out. Why didn't you speak? I could have given you heaps of lights, and you might even have sacrificed another scrap of that precious manuscript."

"Well, she has got a knack of hiding my matches all the same," said Lancelot somewhat shamefacedly. "Besides, I hate her for being called Mary Ann. It's the last terror of cheap apartments. If she only had another name like a human being, I'd gladly call her Miss something. I went so far as to ask her, and she stared at me in a dazed, stupid, silly way, as if I'd asked her to marry me. I suppose the fact is, she's been called Mary Ann so long and so often that she's forgotten her father's name—if she ever had any. I must do her the justice, though, to say she answers to the name of Mary Ann in every sense of the phrase."

"She didn't seem at all bad-looking, any way," said Peter.

"Every man to his taste!" growled Lancelot. "She's as platt and uninteresting as a wooden sabot."

"There's many a pretty foot in a sabot," retorted Peter, with an air of philosophy.

"You think that's clever, but it's simply silly. How does that fact affect this particular sabot?"

"I've put my foot in it," groaned Peter comically.

"Besides, she might be a houri from heaven," said Lancelot; "but a houri in a patched print-frock—" He shuddered, and struck a match.

"I don't know exactly what houris from heaven are, but I have a kind of feeling any sort of frock would be out of harmony—!"

Lancelot lit his pipe.

"If you begin to say that sort of thing, we must smoke," he said, laughing between the puffs. "I can offer you lots of tobacco—I'm sorry I've got no cigars. Wait till you see Mrs. Leadbatter—my landlady—then you'll talk about houris. Poverty may not be a crime, but it seems to make people awful bores. Wonder if it'll have that effect on me? Ach Himmel! how that woman bores me. No, there's no denying it—there's my pouch, old man—I hate the poor; their virtues are only a shade more vulgar than their vices. This Leadbatter creature is honest after her lights—she sends me up the most ridiculous leavings—and I only hate her the more for it."

"I suppose she works Mary Ann's fingers to the bone from the same mistaken sense of duty," said Peter acutely. "Thanks; think I'll try one of my cigars. I filled my case, I fancy, before I came out. Yes, here it is; won't you try one?"

"No, thanks, I prefer my pipe."

"It's the same old meerschaum, I see," said Peter.

"The same old meerschaum," repeated Lancelot, with a little sigh.

Peter lit a cigar, and they sat and puffed in silence.

"Dear me!" said Peter suddenly; "I can almost fancy we're back in our German garret, up the ninety stairs, can't you?"

"No," said Lancelot sadly, looking round as if in search of something; "I miss the dreams."

"And I," said Peter, striving to speak cheerfully, "I see a dog too much."

"Yes," said Lancelot, with a melancholy laugh. "When you funked becoming a Beethoven, I got a dog and called him after you."

"What? you called him Peter?"

"No, Beethoven!"

"Beethoven! Really?"

"Really. Here, Beethoven!"

The spaniel shook himself, and perked his wee nose up wistfully towards Lancelot's face.

Peter laughed, with a little catch in his voice. He didn't know whether he was pleased, or touched, or angry.

"You started to tell me about those twenty thousand shillings," he said.

"Didn't I tell you? On the expectations of my triumph, I lived extravagantly, like a fool, joined a club, and took up my quarters there. When I began to realise the struggle that lay before me, I took chambers; then I took rooms; now I'm in lodgings. The more I realised it, the less rent I paid. I only go to the club for my letters now. I won't have them come here. I'm living incognito."

"That's taking fame by the forelock, indeed! Then by what name must I ask for you next time? For I'm not to be shaken off."

"Lancelot."

"Lancelot what?"

"Only Lancelot! Mr. Lancelot."

"Why, that's like your Mary Ann!"

"So it is!" he laughed, more bitterly than cordially; "it never struck me before. Yes, we are a pair."

"How did you stumble on this place?"

"I didn't stumble. Deliberate, intelligent selection. You see, it's the next best thing to Piccadilly. You just cross Waterloo Bridge, and there you are at the centre, five minutes from all the clubs. The natives have not yet risen to the idea."

"You mean the rent," laughed Peter. "You're as canny and careful as a Scotch professor. I think it's simply grand the way you've beaten out those shillings, in defiance of your natural instincts. I should have melted them years ago. I believe you have got some musical genius, after all."

"You overrate my abilities," said Lancelot, with the whimsical expression that sometimes flashed across his face even in his most unamiable moments. "You must deduct the Thalers I made in exhibitions. As for living in cheap lodgings, I am not at all certain it's an economy, for every now and again it occurs to you that you are saving an awful lot, and you take a hansom on the strength of it."

"Well, I haven't torn up that cheque yet—"

"Peter!" said Lancelot, his flash of gaiety dying away, "I tell you these things as a friend, not as a beggar. If you look upon me as the second, I cease to be the first."

"But, man, I owe you the money; and if it will enable you to hold out a little longer—why, in heaven's name, shouldn't you—?"

"You don't owe me the money at all; I made no bargain with you; I am not a money-lender."

"Pack dich zum Henker!" growled Peter, with a comical grimace. "Was für a casuist! What a swindler you'd make! I wonder you have the face to deny the debt. Well, and how did you leave Frau Sauer-Kraut?" he said, deeming it prudent to sheer off the subject.

"Fat as a Christmas turkey."

"Of a German sausage. The extraordinary things that woman stuffed herself with. Chunks of fat, stewed apples, Kartoffel salad—all mixed up in one plate, as in a dustbin."

"Don't! You make my gorge rise. Ach Himmel! to think that this nation should be musical! O Music, heavenly maid, how much garlic I have endured for thy sake!"

"Ha! ha! ha!" laughed Peter, putting down his whisky that he might throw himself freely back in the easy-chair and roar.

"Oh that garlic!" he said, panting. "No wonder they smoked so much in Leipsic. Even so they couldn't keep the reek out of the staircases. Still, it's a great country is Germany. Our house does a tremendous business in German patents."

"A great country? A land of barbarians rather. How can a people be civilised that eats jam with its meat?"

"Bravo, Lancelot! You're in lovely form to-night. You seem to go a hundred miles out of your way to come the truly British. First it was oil—now it's jam. There was that aristocratic flash in your eye, too, that look of supreme disdain which brings on riots in Trafalgar Square. Behind the patriotic, the national note: 'How can a people be civilised that eats jam with its meat?' I heard the deeper, the oligarchic accent: 'How can a people be enfranchised that eats meat with its fingers?' Ah, you are right! How you do hate the poor! What bores they are! You aristocrats—the products of centuries of culture, comfort, and cocksureness—will never rid yourselves of your conviction that you are the backbone of England—no, not though that backbone were picked clean of every scrap of flesh by the rats of Radicalism."

"What in the devil are you talking about now?" demanded Lancelot. "You seem to me to go a hundred miles out of your way to twit me with my poverty and my breeding. One would almost think you were anxious to convince me of the poverty of your breeding."

"Oh, a thousand pardons!" ejaculated Peter, blushing violently. "But, good heavens, old chap! There's your hot temper again. You surely wouldn't suspect me, of all people in the world, of meaning anything personal? I'm talking of you as a class. Contempt is in your blood—and quite right! We're such snobs, we deserve it. Why d'ye think I ever took to you as a boy at school? Was it because you scribbled inaccurate sonatas and I had myself a talent for knocking tunes off the piano? Not a bit of it. I thought it was, perhaps, but that was only one of my many youthful errors. No, I liked you because your father was an old English baronet, and mine was a merchant who trafficked mainly in things Teutonic. And that's why I like you still. 'Pon my soul it is. You gratify my historic sense—like an old building. You are picturesque. You stand to me for all the good old ideals, including the pride which we are beginning to see is deuced unchristian. Mind you, it's a curious kind of pride when one looks into it. Apparently it's based on the fact that your family has lived on the nation for generations. And yet you won't take my cheque, which is your own. Now don't swear—I know one mustn't analyse things, or the world would come to pieces, so I always vote Tory."

"Then I shall have to turn Radical," grumbled Lancelot.

"Certainly you will, when you have had a little more experience of poverty," retorted Peter. "There, there, old man! forgive me. I only do it to annoy you. Fact is, your outbursts of temper attract me. They are pleasant to look back upon when the storm is over. Yes, my dear Lancelot, you are like the king you look—you can do no wrong. You are picturesque. Pass the whisky."

Lancelot smiled, his handsome brow serene once more. He murmured, "Don't talk rot," but inwardly he was not displeased at Peter's allegiance, half mocking though he knew it.

"Therefore, my dear chap," resumed Peter, sipping his whisky and water, "to return to our lambs, I bow to your patrician prejudices in favour of forks. But your patriotic prejudices are on a different level. There, I am on the same ground as you, and I vow I see nothing inherently superior in the British combination of beef and beetroot, to the German amalgam of lamb and jam."

"Damn lamb and jam," burst forth Lancelot, adding, with his whimsical look: "There's rhyme, as well as reason. How on earth did we get on this tack?"

"I don't know," said Peter, smiling. "We were talking about Frau Sauer-Kraut, I think. And did you board with her all the time?"

"Yes, and I was always hungry. Till the last, I never learnt to stomach her mixtures. But it was really too much trouble to go down the ninety stairs to a restaurant. It was much easier to be hungry."

"And did you ever get a reform in the hours of washing the floor?"

"Ha! ha! ha! No, they always waited till I was going to bed. I suppose they thought I liked damp. They never got over my morning tub, you know. And that, too, sprang a leak after you left, and helped spontaneously to wash the floor."

"Shows the fallacy of cleanliness," said Peter, "and the inferiority of British ideals. They never bathed in their lives, yet they looked the pink of health."

"Yes—their complexion was high—like the fish."

"Ha! ha! Yes, the fish! That was a great luxury, I remember. About once a month."

"Of course, the town is so inland," said Lancelot.

"I see—it took such a long time coming. Ha! ha! ha! And the Herr Professor—is he still a bachelor?"

As the Herr Professor was a septuagenarian and a misogamist, even in Peter's time, his question tickled Lancelot. Altogether the two young men grew quite jolly, recalling a hundred oddities, and reknitting their friendship at the expense of the Fatherland.

"But was there ever a more madcap expedition than ours?" exclaimed Peter. "Most boys start out to be pirates—"

"And some do become music-publishers," Lancelot finished grimly, suddenly reminded of a grievance.

"Ha! ha! ha! Poor fellow'" laughed Peter. "Then you have found them out already."

"Does anyone ever find them in?" flashed Lancelot. "I suppose they do exist and are occasionally seen of mortal eyes. I suppose wives and friends and mothers gaze on them with no sense of special privilege, unconscious of their invisibility to the profane eyes of mere musicians."

"My dear fellow, the mere musicians are as plentiful as niggers on the sea-shore. A publisher might spend his whole day receiving regiments of unappreciated geniuses. Bond Street would be impassable. You look at the publisher too much from your own standpoint."

"I tell you I don't look at him from any standpoint. That's what I complain of. He's encircled with a prickly hedge of clerks. 'You will hear from us.' 'It shall have our best consideration.' 'We have no knowledge of the MS. in question.' Yes, Peter, two valuable quartets have I lost, messing about with these villains."

"I tell you what. I'll give you an introduction to Brahmson. I know him—privately."

"No, thank you, Peter."

"Why not?"

"Because you know him."

"I couldn't give you an introduction if I didn't. This is silly of you, Lancelot."

"If Brahmson can't see any merits in my music, I don't want you to open his eyes. I'll stand on my own bottom. And what's more, Peter, I tell you once for all"—his voice was low and menacing—"if you try any anonymous deus ex machinâ tricks on me in some sly, roundabout fashion, don't you flatter yourself I shan't recognise your hand. I shall, and, by God, it shall never grasp mine again."

"I suppose you think that's very noble and sublime," said Peter coolly. "You don't suppose if I could do you a turn I'd hesitate for fear of excommunication? I know you're like Beethoven there—your bark is worse than your bite."

"Very well; try. You'll find my teeth nastier than you bargain for."

"I'm not going to try. If you want to go to the dogs—go. Why should I put out a hand to stop you?"

These amenities having re-established them in their mutual esteem, they chatted lazily and spasmodically till past midnight, with more smoke than fire in their conversation.

At last Peter began to go, and in course of time actually did take up his umbrella. Not long after, Lancelot conducted him softly down the dark, silent stairs, holding his bedroom candlestick in his hand, for Mrs. Leadbatter always turned out the hall lamp on her way to bed. The old phrases came to the young men's lips as their hands met in a last hearty grip.

"Lebt wohl!" said Lancelot.

"Auf Wiedersehen!" replied Peter threateningly.

Lancelot stood at the hall door looking for a moment after his friend—the friend he had tried to cast out of his heart as a recreant. The mist had cleared—the stars glittered countless in the frosty heaven; a golden crescent moon hung low; the lights and shadows lay almost poetically upon the little street. A rush of tender thoughts whelmed the musician's soul. He saw again the dear old garret, up the ninety stairs, in the Hotel Cologne, where he had lived with his dreams; he heard the pianos and violins going in every room in happy incongruity, publishing to all the prowess of the players; dirty, picturesque old Leipsic rose before him; he was walking again in the Hainstrasse, in the shadow of the quaint, tall houses. Yes, life was sweet after all; he was a coward to lose heart so soon; fame would yet be his; fame and love—the love of a noble woman that fame earns; some gracious creature breathing sweet refinements, cradled in an ancient home, such as he had left for ever.

The sentimentality of the Fatherland seemed to have crept into his soul; a divinely sweet, sad melody was throbbing in his brain. How glad he was he had met Peter again!

From a neighbouring steeple came a harsh, resonant clang, "One."

It roused him from his dream. He shivered a little, closed the door, bolted it and put up the chain, and turned, half sighing, to take up his bedroom candle again. Then his heart stood still for a moment. A figure—a girl's figure—was coming towards him from the kitchen stairs. As she came into the dim light he saw that it was merely Mary Ann.

She looked half drowsed. Her cap was off, her hair tangled loosely over her forehead. In her disarray she looked prettier than he had ever remembered her. There was something provoking about the large dreamy eyes, the red lips that parted at the unexpected sight of him.

"Good heavens!" he cried. "Not gone to bed yet?"

"No, sir. I had to stay up to wash up a lot of crockery. The second-floor front had some friends to supper late. Missus says she won't stand it again."

"Poor thing!" He patted her soft cheek—it grew hot and rosy under his fingers, but was not withdrawn. Mary Ann made no sign of resentment. In his mood of tenderness to all creation his rough words to her recurred to him.

"You mustn't mind what I said about the matches," he murmured. "When I am in a bad temper I say anything. Remember now for the future, will you?"

"Yessir."

Her face—its blushes flickered over strangely by the candle-light—seemed to look up at him invitingly.

"That's a good girl." And bending down he kissed her on the lips.

"Good night," he murmured.

Mary Ann made some startled, gurgling sound in reply.

Five minutes afterwards Lancelot was in bed, denouncing himself as a vulgar beast.

"I must have drunk too much whisky," he said to himself angrily. "Good heavens. Fancy sinking to Mary Ann. If Peter had only seen— There was infinitely more poetry in that red-cheeked Mädchen, and yet I never— It is true—there is something sordid about the atmosphere that subtly permeates you, that drags you down to it! Mary Ann! A transpontine drudge! whose lips are fresh from the coalman's and the butcher's. Phaugh!"

The fancy seized hold of his imagination. He could not shake it off, he could not sleep till he had got out of bed and sponged his lips vigorously.

Meanwhile Mary Ann was lying on her bed, dressed, doing her best to keep her meaningless, half-hysterical sobs from her mistress's keen ear.

II

It was a long time before Mary Ann came so prominently into the centre of Lancelot's consciousness again. She remained somewhere in the outer periphery of his thought—nowhere near the bull's-eye, so to speak—as a vague automaton that worked when he pulled a bell-rope. Infinitely more important things were troubling him; the visit of Peter had somehow put a keener edge on his blunted self-confidence; he had started a grand opera, and worked at it furiously in all the intervals left him by his engrossing pursuit after a publisher. Sometimes he would look up from his hieroglyphics and see Mary Ann at his side surveying him curiously, and then he would start, and remember he had rung her up, and try to remember what for. And Mary Ann would turn red, as if the fault was hers.

But the publisher was the one thing that was never out of Lancelot's mind, though he drove Lancelot himself nearly out of it. He was like an arrow stuck in the aforesaid bull's-eye, and, the target being conscious, he rankled sorely. Lancelot discovered that the publisher kept a "musical adviser," whose advice appeared to consist of the famous monosyllable, "Don't." The publisher generally published all the musical adviser's own works, his advice having apparently been neglected when it was most worth taking; at least so Lancelot thought, when he had skimmed through a set of Lancers by one of these worthies.

"I shall give up being a musician," he said to himself grimly. "I shall become a musical adviser."

Once, half by accident, he actually saw a publisher. "My dear sir," said the great man, "what is the use of bringing quartets and full scores to me? You should have taken them to Brahmson; he's the man you want. You know his address, of course—just down the street."

Lancelot did not like to say that it was Brahmson's clerks that had recommended him here; so he replied, "But you publish operas, oratorios, cantatas!"

"Ah yes!—h'm—things that have been played at the big Festivals—composers of prestige—quite a different thing, sir, quite a different thing. There's no sale for these things—none at all, sir—public never heard of you. Now, if you were to write some songs—nice catchy tunes—high class, you know, with pretty words—"

Now Lancelot by this time was aware of the publisher's wily ways; he could almost have constructed an Ollendorffian dialogue, entitled "Between a Music-Publisher and a Composer." So he opened his portfolio again and said, "I have brought some."

"Well, send—send them in," stammered the publisher, almost disconcerted. "They shall have our best consideration."

"Oh, but you might just as well look over them at once," said Lancelot firmly, uncoiling them. "It won't take you five minutes—just let me play one to you. The tunes are rather more original than the average, I can promise you; and yet I think they have a lilt that—"

"I really can't spare the time now. If you leave them, we will do our best."

"Listen to this bit!" said Lancelot desperately. And dashing at a piano that stood handy, he played a couple of bars. "That's quite a new modulation."

"That's all very well," said the publisher; "but how do you suppose I'm going to sell a thing with an accompaniment like that? Look here, and here! Why it's all accidentals."

"That's the best part of the song," explained Lancelot; "a sort of undercurrent of emotion that brings out the full pathos of the words. Note the elegant and novel harmonies." He played another bar or two, singing the words softly.

"Yes; but if you think you'll get young ladies to play that, you've got a good deal to learn," said the publisher gruffly. "This is the sort of accompaniment that goes down," and seating himself at the piano for a moment (somewhat to Lancelot's astonishment, for he had gradually formed a theory that music-publishers did not really know the staff from a five-barred gate), he rattled off the melody with his right hand, pounding away monotonously with his left at a few elementary chords.

Lancelot looked dismayed.

"That's the kind of thing you'll have to produce, young man," said the publisher, feeling that he had at last resumed his natural supremacy, "if you want to get your songs published. Elegant harmonies are all very well, but who's to play them?"

"And do you mean to say that a musician in this God-forsaken country must have no chords but tonics and dominants?" ejaculated Lancelot hotly.

"The less he has of any other the better," said the great man drily. "I haven't said a word about the melody itself, which is quite out of the ordinary compass, and makes demands upon the singer's vocalisation which are not likely to make a demand for the song. What you have to remember, my dear sir, if you wish to achieve success, is that music, if it is to sell, must appeal to the average amateur young person. The average amateur young person is the main prop of music in this country."

Lancelot snatched up his song and tied the strings of his portfolio very tightly, as if he were clenching his lips.

"If I stay here any longer I shall swear," he said: "Good afternoon."

He went out with a fire at his heart that made him insensitive to the frost without. He walked a mile out of his way mechanically, then, perceiving his stupidity, avenged it by jumping into a hansom. He dared not think how low his funds were running. When he got home he forgot to have his tea, crouching in dumb misery in his easy-chair, while the coals in the grate faded like the sunset from red to grey, and the dusk of twilight deepened into the gloom of night, relieved only by a gleam from the street-lamp.

The noise of the door opening made him look up.

"Beg pardon, sir, I didn't yer ye come in."

It was Mary Ann's timid accents. Lancelot's head drooped again on his breast. He did not answer.

"You've bin and let your fire go out, sir."

"Don't bother!" he grumbled. He felt a morbid satisfaction in this aggravation of discomfort, almost symbolic as it was of his sunk fortunes.

"Oh, but it'll freeze 'ard to-night, sir. Let me make it up." Taking his sullen silence for consent, she ran downstairs and reappeared with some sticks. Soon there were signs of life, which Mary Ann assiduously encouraged by blowing at the embers with her mouth. Lancelot looked on in dull apathy, but as the fire rekindled and the little flames leapt up and made Mary Ann's flushed face the one spot of colour and warmth in the cold, dark room, Lancelot's torpidity vanished suddenly. The sensuous fascination seized him afresh, and ere he was aware of it he was lifting the pretty face by the chin.

"I'm so sorry to be so troublesome, Mary Ann. There, you shall give me a kiss to show you bear no malice."

The warm lips obediently met his, and for a moment Lancelot forgot his worries while he held her soft cheek against his.

This time the shock of returning recollection was not so violent as before. He sat up in his chair, but his right arm still twined negligently round her neck, the fingers patting the warm face. "A fellow must have something to divert his mind," he thought, "or he'd go mad. And there's no harm done—the poor thing takes it as a kindness, I'm sure. I suppose her life's dull enough. We're a pair." He felt her shoulders heaving a little, as if she were gulping down something. At last she said, "You ain't troublesome. I ought to ha' yerd ye come in."

He released her suddenly. Her words broke the spell. The vulgar accent gave him a shudder.

"Don't you hear a bell ringing?" he said, with dual significance.

"Nosir," said Mary Ann ingenuously. "I'd yer it in a moment if there was. I yer it in my dreams, I'm so used to it. One night I dreamt the missus was boxin' my yers and askin' me if I was deaf and I said to 'er—"

"Can't you say 'her'?" cried Lancelot, cutting her short impatiently.

"Her," said Mary Ann.

"Then why do you say ''er'?"

"Missus told me to. She said my own way was all wrong."

"Oh, indeed!" said Lancelot. "It's missus that has corrupted you, is it? And pray what used you to say?"

"She," said Mary Ann.

Lancelot was taken aback. "She!" he repeated.

"Yessir," said Mary Ann, with a dawning suspicion that her own vocabulary was going to be vindicated; "whenever I said 'she' she made me say ''er,' and whenever I said 'her' she made me say 'she.' When I said 'her and me' she made me say 'me and she,' and when I said 'I got it from she,' she made me say 'I got it from 'er.'"

"Bravo! A very lucid exposition," said Lancelot, laughing. "Did she set you right in any other particulars?"

"Eessir—I mean yessir," replied Mary Ann, the forbidden words flying to her lips like prisoned skylarks suddenly set free. "I used to say, 'Gie I thek there broom, oo't?' 'Arten thee goin' to?' 'Her did say to I.' 'I be goin' on to bed.' 'Look at—'"

"Enough! Enough! What a memory you've got! Now I understand. You're a country girl."

"Eessir," said Mary Ann, her face lighting up. "I mean yessir."

"Well, that redeems you a little," thought Lancelot, with his whimsical look. "So it's missus, is it, who's taught you Cockneyese? My instinct was not so unsound, after all. I dare say you'll turn out something nobler than a Cockney drudge." He finished aloud, "I hope you went a-milking."

"Eessir, sometimes; and I drove back the milk-trunk in the cart, and I rode down on a pony to the second pasture to count the sheep and the heifers."

"Then you are a farmer's daughter?"

"Eessir. But my feyther—I mean my father—had only two little fields when he was alive, but we had a nice garden, with plum trees, and rose bushes and gillyflowers—"

"Better and better," murmured Lancelot, smiling. And, indeed, the image of Mary Ann skimming the meads on a pony in the sunshine was more pleasant to contemplate than that of Mary Ann whitening the wintry steps. "What a complexion you must have had to start with!" he cried aloud, surveying the not unenviable remains of it. "Well, and what else did you do?"

Mary Ann opened her lips. It was delightful to see how the dull veil, as of London fog, had been lifted from her face; her eyes sparkled.

Then, "Oh, there's the ground-floor bell," she cried, moving instinctively towards the door.

"Nonsense: I hear no bell," said Lancelot.

"I told you I always hear it," said Mary Ann, hesitating and blushing delicately before the critical word.

"Oh well, run along then. Stop a moment—I must give you another kiss for talking so nicely. There! And—stop a moment—bring me up some coffee, please, when the ground floor is satisfied."

"Eessir—I mean yessir. What must I say?" she added, pausing troubled on the threshold.

"Say, 'Yes, Lancelot,'" he answered recklessly.

"Yessir," and Mary Ann disappeared.

It was ten endless minutes before she reappeared with the coffee. The whole of the second five minutes Lancelot paced his room feverishly, cursing the ground floor, and stamping as if to bring down its ceiling. He was curious to know more of Mary Ann's history.

But it proved meagre enough. Her mother died when Mary Ann was a child; her father when she was still a mere girl. His affairs were found in hopeless confusion, and Mary Ann was considered lucky to be taken into the house of the well-to-do Mrs. Leadbatter, of London, the eldest sister of a young woman who had nursed the vicar's wife. Mrs. Leadbatter had promised the vicar to train up the girl in the way a domestic should go.

"And when I am old enough she is going to pay me wages as well," concluded Mary Ann, with an air of importance.

"Indeed—how old were you when you left the village?"

"Fourteen."

"And how old are you now?"

Mary Ann looked confused. "I don't quite know," she murmured.

"O come," said Lancelot laughingly; "is this your country simplicity? You're quite young enough to tell how old you are."

The tears came into Mary Ann's eyes.

"I can't, Mr. Lancelot," she protested earnestly; "I forgot to count—I'll ask missus."

"And whatever she tells you, you'll be," he said, amused at her unshakable loyalty.

"Yessir," said Mary Ann.

"And so you are quite alone in the world?"

"Yessir—but I've got my canary. They sold everything when my father died, but the vicar's wife she bought my canary back for me because I cried so. And I brought it to London and it hangs in my bedroom. And the vicar, he was so kind to me, he did give me a lot of advice, and Mrs. Amersham, who kept the chandler's shop, she did give me ninepence, all in three-penny bits."

"And you never had any brothers or sisters?"

"There was our Sally, but she died before mother."

"Nobody else?"

"There's my big brother Tom—but I mustn't tell you about him."

"Mustn't tell me about him? Why not?"

"He's so wicked."

The answer was so unexpected that Lancelot, could not help laughing, and Mary Ann flushed to the roots of her hair.

"Why, what has he done?" said Lancelot, composing his mouth to gravity.

"I don't know; I was only six. Father told me it was something very dreadful, and Tom had to run away to America, and I mustn't mention him any more. And mother was crying, and I cried because Tom used to give me tickey-backs and go blackberrying with me and our little Sally; and everybody else in the village they seemed glad, because they had said so all along, because Tom would never go to church, even when a little boy."

"I suppose then you went to church regularly?"

"Yessir. When I was at home, I mean."

"Every Sunday?"

Mary Ann hung her head. "Once I went meechin'," she said in low tones. "Some boys and girls they wanted me to go nutting, and I wanted to go too, but I didn't know how to get away, and they told me to cough very loud when the sermon began, so I did, and coughed on and on till at last the vicar glowed at father, and father had to send me out of church."

Lancelot laughed heartily. "Then you didn't like the sermon."

"It wasn't that, sir. The sun was shining that beautiful outside, and I never minded the sermon, only I did get tired of sitting still. But I never done it again—our little Sally, she died soon after."

Lancelot checked his laughter. "Poor little fool!" he thought. Then to brighten her up again he asked cheerily, "And what else did you do on the farm?"

"Oh, please sir, missus will be wanting me now."

"Bother missus. I want some more milk," he said, emptying the milk-jug into the slop-basin. "Run down and get some."

Mary Ann was startled by the splendour of the deed. She took the jug silently and disappeared.

When she returned he said: "Well, you haven't told me half yet. I suppose you kept bees?"

"Oh yes, and I fed the pigs."

"Hang the pigs! Let's hear something more romantic."

"There was the calves to suckle sometimes, when the mother died or was sold."

"Calves! H'm! H'm! Well, but how could you do that?"

"Dipped my fingers in milk, and let the calves suck 'em. The silly creatures thought it was their mothers' teats. Like this."

With a happy inspiration she put her fingers into the slop-basin, and held them up dripping.

Lancelot groaned. It was not only that his improved Mary Ann was again sinking to earth, unable to soar in the romantic aether where he would fain have seen her volant; it was not only that the coarseness of her nature had power to drag her down, it was the coarseness of her red, chapped hands that was thrust once again and violently upon his reluctant consciousness.

Then, like Mary Ann, he had an inspiration.

"How would you like a pair of gloves, Mary Ann?"

He had struck the latent feminine. Her eyes gleamed. "Oh, sir!" was all she could say. Then a swift shade of disappointment darkened the eager little face.

"But I never goes out," she cried.

"I never go out," he corrected, shuddering.

"I never go out," said Mary Ann, her lip twitching.

"That doesn't matter. I want you to wear them indoors."

"But there's nobody to see 'em indoors!"

"I shall see them," he reminded her.

"But they'll get dirty."

"No they won't. You shall only wear them when you come to me. If I buy you a nice pair of gloves, will you promise to put them on every time I ring for you?"

"But what'll missus say?"

"Missus won't see them. The moment you come in, you'll put them on, and just before going out—you'll take them off! See!"

"Yessir. Then nobody'll see me looking so grand but you."

"That's it. And wouldn't you rather look grand for me than for anybody else?"

"Of course I would, sir," said Mary Ann, earnestly, with a grateful little sigh.

So Lancelot measured her wrist, feeling her pulse beat madly. She really had a very little hand, though to his sensitive vision the roughness of the skin seemed to swell it to a size demanding a boxing-glove. He bought her six pairs of tan kid, in a beautiful cardboard box. He could ill afford the gift, and made one of his whimsical grimaces when he got the bill. The young lady who served him looked infinitely more genteel than Mary Ann. He wondered what she would think if she knew for whom he was buying these dainty articles. Perhaps her feelings would be so outraged she would refuse to participate in the transaction. But the young lady was happily unconscious; she had her best smile for the handsome, aristocratic young gentleman, and mentioned his moustache later to her bosom-friend in the next department.

And thus Mary Ann and Lancelot became the joint owners of a secret, and co-players in a little comedy. When Mary Ann came into the room, she would put whatever she was carrying on a chair, gravely extract her gloves from her pocket, and draw them on, Lancelot pretending not to know she was in the room, though he had just said, "Come in." After allowing her a minute he would look up. In the course of a week this became mechanical, so that he lost the semi-ludicrous sense of secrecy which he felt at first, as well as the little pathetic emotion inspired by her absolute unconsciousness that the performance was not intended for her own gratification. Nevertheless, though he could now endure to see Mary Ann handling the sugar-tongs, he remained cold to her for some weeks. He had kissed her again in the flush of her joy at the sight of the gloves, but after that there was a reaction. He rarely went to the club now (there was no one with whom he was in correspondence except music-publishers, and they didn't reply), but he dropped in there once soon after the glove episode, looked over the papers in the smoking-room, and chatted with a popular composer and one or two men he knew. It was while the waiter was holding out the coffee-tray to him that Mary Ann flashed upon his consciousness. The thought of her seemed so incongruous with the sober magnificence, the massive respectability that surrounded him, the cheerful, marble hearth reddened with leaping flame, the luxurious lounges, the well-groomed old gentlemen smoking eighteenpenny cheroots, the suave, noiseless satellites, that Lancelot felt a sudden pang of bewildered shame. Why, the very waiter who stood bent before him would disdain her. He took his coffee hastily, with a sense of personal unworthiness. This feeling soon evaporated, but it left lees of resentment against Mary Ann which made him inexplicable to her. Fortunately, her habit of acceptance saved her some tears, though she shed others. And there remained always the gloves. When she was putting them on she always felt she was slipping her hands in his.

And then there was yet a further consolation. For the gloves had also a subtle effect on Lancelot. They gave him a sense of responsibility. Vaguely resentful as he felt against Mary Ann (in the intervals of his more definite resentment against publishers), he also felt that he could not stop at the gloves. He had started refining her, and he must go on till she was, so to speak, all gloves. He must cover up her coarse speech, as he had covered up her coarse hands. He owed that to the gloves; it was the least he could do for them. So, whenever Mary Ann made a mistake, Lancelot corrected her. He found these grammatical dialogues not uninteresting, and a vent for his ill-humour against publishers to boot. Very often his verbal corrections sounded astonishingly like reprimands. Here, again, Mary Ann was forearmed by her feeling that she deserved them. She would have been proud had she known how much Mr. Lancelot was satisfied with her aspirates, which came quite natural. She had only dropped her "h's" temporarily, as one drops country friends in coming to London. Curiously enough, Mary Ann did not regard the new locutions and pronunciations as superseding the old. They were a new language; she knew two others, her mother-tongue and her missus's tongue. She would as little have thought of using her new linguistic acquirements in the kitchen as of wearing her gloves there. They were for Lancelot's ears only, as her gloves were for his eyes.

All this time Lancelot was displaying prodigious musical activity, so much so that the cost of ruled paper became a consideration. There was no form of composition he did not essay, none by which he made a shilling. Once he felt himself the prey of a splendid inspiration, and sat up all night writing at fever pitch, surrounded with celestial harmonies, audible to him alone; the little room resounded with the thunder of a mighty orchestra, in which every instrument sang to him individually—the piccolo, the flute, the oboes, the clarionets, filling the air with a silver spray of notes; the drums throbbing, the trumpets shrilling, the four horns pealing with long, stately notes, the trombones and bassoons vibrating, the violins and violas sobbing in linked sweetness, the 'cello and the contra-bass moaning their under-chant. And then, in the morning, when the first rough sketch was written, the glory faded. He threw down his pen, and called himself an ass for wasting his time on what nobody would ever look at. Then he laid his head on the table, overwrought, full of an infinite pity for himself. A sudden longing seized him for some one to love him, to caress his hair, to smooth his hot forehead. This mood passed too; he smoothed the slumbering Beethoven instead. After a while he went into his bedroom, and sluiced his face and hands in ice-cold water, and rang the bell for breakfast.

There was a knock at the door in response.

"Come in!" he said gently—his emotions had left him tired to the point of tenderness. And then he waited a minute while Mary Ann was drawing on her gloves.

"Did you ring, sir?" said a wheezy voice at last. Mrs. Leadbatter had got tired of waiting.

Lancelot started violently—Mrs. Leadbatter had latterly left him entirely to Mary Ann. "It's my hastmer," she had explained to him apologetically, meeting him casually in the passage. "I can't trollop up and down stairs as I used to when I fust took this house five-an'-twenty year ago, and pore Mr. Leadbatter—" and here followed reminiscences long since in their hundredth edition.

"Yes; let me have some coffee—very hot—please," said Lancelot less gently. The woman's voice jarred upon him; and her features were not redeeming.

"Lawd, sir, I 'ope that gas 'asn't been burnin' all night, sir," she said as she was going out.

"It has," he said shortly.

"You'll hexcoose me, sir, but I didn't bargen for that. I'm only a pore, honest, 'ard-workin' widder, and I noticed the last gas bill was 'eavier than hever since that black winter that took pore Mr. Leadbatter to 'is grave. Fair is fair, and I shall 'ave to reckon it a hextry, with the rate gone up sevenpence a thousand, and my Rosie leavin' a fine nursemaid's place in Bayswater at the end of the month to come 'ome and 'elp 'er mother, 'cos my hastmer—"

"Will you please shut the door after you?" interrupted Lancelot, biting his lip with irritation. And Mrs. Leadbatter, who was standing in the aperture with no immediate intention of departing, could find no repartee beyond slamming the door as hard as she could.

This little passage of arms strangely softened Lancelot to Mary Ann. It made him realise faintly what her life must be.

"I should go mad and smash all the crockery!" he cried aloud. He felt quite tender again towards the uncomplaining girl.

Presently there was another knock. Lancelot growled, half prepared to renew the battle, and to give Mrs. Leadbatter a piece of his mind on the subject. But it was merely Mary Ann.

Shaken in his routine, he looked on steadily while Mary Ann drew on her gloves; and this in turn confused Mary Ann. Her hand trembled.

"Let me help you," he said.

And there was Lancelot buttoning Mary Ann's glove just as if her name were Guinevere! And neither saw the absurdity of wasting time upon an operation which would have to be undone in two minutes. Then Mary Ann, her eyes full of soft light, went to the sideboard and took out the prosaic elements of breakfast.

When she returned, to put them back, Lancelot was astonished to see her carrying a cage—a plain square cage, made of white tin wire.

"What's that?" he gasped.

"Please, Mr. Lancelot, I want to ask you to do me a favour." She dropped her eyelashes timidly.

"Yes, Mary Ann," he said briskly. "But what have you got there?"

"It's only my canary, sir. Would you—please, sir, would you mind?"—then desperately: "I want to hang it up here, sir!"

"Here?" he repeated in frank astonishment.

"Why?"

"Please, sir, I—I—it's sunnier here, sir, and I—I think it must be pining away. It hardly ever sings in my bedroom."

"Well, but," he began—then seeing the tears gathering on her eyelids, he finished with laughing good-nature—"as long as Mrs. Leadbatter doesn't reckon it an extra."

"Oh no, sir," said Mary Ann seriously. "I'll tell her. Besides, she will be glad, because she don't like the canary—she says its singing disturbs her. Her room is next to mine, you know, Mr. Lancelot."

"But you said it doesn't sing much."

"Please, sir, I—I mean in summer," exclaimed Mary Ann in rosy confusion; "and—and—it'll soon be summer, sir."

"Sw—e-ê-t!" burst forth the canary suddenly, as if encouraged by Mary Ann's opinion. It was a pretty little bird—one golden yellow from beak to tail, as though it had been dipped in sunshine.

"You see, sir," she cried eagerly, "it's beginning already."

"Yes," said Lancelot grimly; "but so is Beethoven."

"I'll hang it high up—in the window," said Mary Ann, "where the dog can't get at it."

"Well, I won't take any responsibilities," murmured Lancelot resignedly.

"No, sir, I'll attend to that," said Mary Ann vaguely.

After the installation of the canary Lancelot found himself slipping more and more into a continuous matter-of-course flirtation; more and more forgetting the slavey in the candid young creature who had, at moments, strange dancing lights in her awakened eyes, strange flashes of witchery in her ingenuous expression. And yet he made a desultory struggle against what a secret voice was always whispering was a degradation. He knew she had no real place in his life; he scarce thought of her save when she came bodily before his eyes with her pretty face and her trustful glance.

He felt no temptation to write sonatas on her eyebrow—to borrow Peter's variation, for the use of musicians, of Shakespeare's "write sonnets on his mistress's eyebrow"—and, indeed, he knew she could be no fit mistress for him—this starveling drudge, with passive passions, meek, accepting, with well-nigh every spark of spontaneity choked out of her. The women of his dreams were quite other—beautiful, voluptuous, full of the joy of life, tremulous with poetry and lofty thought, with dark, amorous orbs that flashed responsive to his magic melodies. They hovered about him as he wrote and played—Venuses rising from the seas of his music. And then—with his eyes full of the divine tears of youth, with his brain a hive of winged dreams—he would turn and kiss merely Mary Ann! Such is the pitiful breed of mortals.

And after every such fall he thought more contemptuously of Mary Ann. Idealise her as he might, see all that was best in her as he tried to do, she remained common and commonplace enough. Her ingenuousness, while from one point of view it was charming, from another was but a pleasant synonym for silliness. And it might not be ingenuousness—or silliness—after all! For was Mary Ann as innocent as she looked? The guilelessness of the dove might very well cover the wisdom of the serpent. The instinct—the repugnance that made him sponge off her first kiss from his lips—was probably a true instinct. How was it possible a girl of that class should escape the sordid attentions of street swains? Even when she was in the country she was well-nigh of woo-able age, the likely cynosure of neighbouring ploughboys' eyes. And what of the other lodgers?

A finer instinct—that of a gentleman—kept him from putting any questions to Mary Ann. Indeed, his own delicacy repudiated the images that strove to find entry in his brain, even as his fastidiousness shrank from realising the unlovely details of Mary Ann's daily duties—these things disgusted him more with himself than with her. And yet he found himself acquiring a new and illogical interest in the boots he met outside doors. Early one morning he went half-way up the second flight of stairs—a strange region where his own boots had never before trod—but came down ashamed and with fluttering heart as if he had gone up to steal boots instead of to survey them. He might have asked Mary Ann or her "missus" who the other tenants were, but he shrank from the topic. Their hours were not his, and he only once chanced on a fellow-man in the passage, and then he was not sure it was not the tax-collector. Besides, he was not really interested—it was only a flicker of idle curiosity as to the actual psychology of Mary Ann. That he did not really care he proved to himself by kissing her next time. He accepted her as she was—because she was there. She brightened his troubled life a little, and he was quite sure he brightened hers. So he drifted on, not worrying himself to mean any definite harm to her. He had quite enough worry with those music-publishers.

The financial outlook was, indeed, becoming terrifying. He was glad there was nobody to question him, for he did not care to face the facts. Peter's threat of becoming a regular visitor had been nullified by his father despatching him to Germany to buy up some more Teutonic patents. "Wonderful are the ways of Providence!" he had written to Lancelot. "If I had not flown in the old man's face and picked up a little German here years ago, I should not be half so useful to him now. . . . I shall pay a flying visit to Leipsic—not on business."

But at last Peter returned, Mrs. Leadbatter panting to the door to let him in one afternoon without troubling to ask Lancelot if he was "at home." He burst upon the musician, and found him in the most undisguisable dumps.

"Why didn't you answer my letter, you impolite old bear?" Peter asked, warding off Beethoven with his umbrella.

"I was busy," Lancelot replied pettishly.

"Busy writing rubbish. Haven't you got 'Ops.' enough? I bet you haven't had anything published yet."

"I'm working at a grand opera," he said in dry, mechanical tones. "I have hopes of getting it put on. Gasco, the impresario, is a member of my club, and he thinks of running a season in the autumn. I had a talk with him yesterday."

"I hope I shall live to see it," said Peter sceptically.

"I hope you will," said Lancelot sharply.

"None of my family ever lived beyond ninety," said Peter, shaking his head dolefully; "and then, my heart is not so good as it might be."

"It certainly isn't!" cried poor Lancelot. "But everybody hits a chap when he's down."

He turned his head away, striving to swallow the lump that would rise to his throat. He had a sense of infinite wretchedness and loneliness.

"Oh, poor old chap; is it so bad as all that?" Peter's somewhat strident voice had grown tender as a woman's. He laid his hand affectionately on Lancelot's tumbled hair. "You know I believe in you with all my soul. I never doubted your genius for a moment. Don't I know too well that's what keeps you back? Come, come, old fellow. Can't I persuade you to write rot? One must keep the pot boiling, you know. You turn out a dozen popular ballads, and the coin'll follow your music as the rats did the pied piper's. Then, if you have any ambition left, you kick away the ladder by which you mounted, and stand on the heights of art."

"Never!" cried Lancelot. "It would degrade me in my own eyes. I'd rather starve; and you can't shake them off—the first impression is everything; they would always be remembered against me," he added, after a pause.

"Motives mixed," reflected Peter. "That's a good sign." Aloud he said, "Well, you think it over. This is a practical world, old man; it wasn't made for dreamers. And one of the first dreams that you've got to wake from is the dream that anybody connected with the stage can be relied on from one day to the next. They gas for the sake of gassing, or they tell you pleasant lies out of mere goodwill, just as they call for your drinks. Their promises are beautiful bubbles, on a basis of soft soap and made to 'bust.'"

"You grow quite eloquent," said Lancelot, with a wan smile.

"Eloquent! There's more in me than you've yet found out. Now, then! Give us your hand that you'll chuck art, and we'll drink to your popular ballad—hundredth thousand edition, no drawing-room should be without it."

Lancelot flushed. "I was just going to have some tea. I think it's five o'clock," he murmured.

"The very thing I'm dying for," cried Peter energetically; "I'm as parched as a pea." Inwardly he was shocked to find the stream of whisky run dry.

So Lancelot rang the bell, and Mary Ann came up with the tea-tray in the twilight.

"We'll have a light," cried Peter, and struck one of his own with a shadowy underthought of saving Mary Ann from a possible scolding, in case Lancelot's matches should be again unapparent. Then he uttered a comic exclamation of astonishment. Mary Ann was putting on a pair of gloves! In his surprise he dropped the match.

Mary Ann was equally startled by the unexpected sight of a stranger, but when he struck the second match her hands were bare and red.

"What in heaven's name were you putting on gloves for, my girl?" said Peter, amused.

Lancelot stared fixedly at the fire, trying to keep the blood from flooding his cheeks. He wondered that the ridiculousness of the whole thing had never struck him in its full force before. Was it possible he could have made such an ass of himself?

"Please, sir, I've got to go out, and I'm in a hurry," said Mary Ann.

Lancelot felt intense relief. An instant after his brow wrinkled itself. "Oho!" he thought. "So this is Miss Simpleton, is it?"

"Then why did you take them off again?" retorted Peter.

Mary Ann's repartee was to burst into tears and leave the room.

"Now I've offended her," said Peter. "Did you see how she tossed her pretty head?"

"Ingenious minx," thought Lancelot.

"She's left the tray on a chair by the door," went on Peter. "What an odd girl! Does she always carry on like this?"

"She's got such a lot to do. I suppose she sometimes gets a bit queer in her head," said Lancelot, conceiving he was somehow safe-guarding Mary Ann's honour by the explanation.

"I don't think tnat," answered Peter. "She did seem dull and stupid when I was here last. But I had a good stare at her just now, and she seems rather bright. Why, her accent is quite refined—she must have picked it up from you."

"Nonsense, nonsense!" exclaimed Lancelot testily.

The little danger—or rather the great danger of being made to appear ridiculous—which he had just passed through, contributed to rouse him from his torpor. He exerted himself to turn the conversation, and was quite lively over tea.

"Sw—eêt! Sw—w—w—w—eêt!" suddenly broke into the conversation.

"More mysteries!" cried Peter. "What's that?"

"Only a canary."

"What, another musical instrument! Isn't Beethoven jealous? I wonder he doesn't consume his rival in his wrath. But I never knew you liked birds."

"I don't particularly. It isn't mine."

"Whose is it?"

Lancelot answered briskly, "Mary Ann's. She asked to be allowed to keep it here. It seems it won't sing in her attic; it pines away."

"And do you believe that?"

"Why not? It doesn't sing much even here."

"Let me look at it—ah, it's a plain Norwich yellow. If you wanted a singing canary you should have come to me, I'd have given you one 'made in Germany'—one of our patents—they train them to sing tunes, and that puts up the price."

"Thank you, but this one disturbs me sufficiently."

"Then why do you put up with it?"

"Why do I put up with that Christmas number supplement over the mantel-piece? It's part of the furniture. I was asked to let it be here, and I couldn't be rude."

"No, it's not in your nature. What a bore it must be to feed it! Let me see, I suppose you give it canary seed biscuits—I hope you don't give it butter."

"Don't be an ass!" roared Lancelot. "You don't imagine I bother my head whether it eats butter or—or marmalade."

"Who feeds it then?"

"Mary Ann, of course."

"She comes in and feeds it?"

"Certainly."

"Several times a day?"

"I suppose so."

"Lancelot," said Peter solemnly, "Mary Ann's mashed on you."

Lancelot shrank before Peter's remark as a burglar from a policeman's bull's-eye. The bull's-eye seemed to cast a new light on Mary Ann, too, but he felt too unpleasantly dazzled to consider that for the moment; his whole thought was to get out of the line of light.

"Nonsense!" he answered; "why I'm hardly ever in when she feeds it, and I believe it eats all day long—gets supplied in the morning like a coal-scuttle. Besides, she comes in to dust and all that when she pleases. And I do wish you wouldn't use that word 'mashed.' I loathe it."

Indeed, he writhed under the thought of being coupled with Mary Ann. The thing sounded so ugly—so squalid. In the actual, it was not so unpleasant, but looked at from the outside—unsympathetically—it was hopelessly vulgar, incurably plebeian. He shuddered.

"I don't know," said Peter. "It's a very expressive word, is 'mashed.' But I will make allowance for your poetical feelings and give up the word—except in its literal sense, of course. I'm sure you wouldn't object to mashing a music-publisher!"

Lancelot laughed with false heartiness. "Oh, but if I'm to write those popular ballads, you say he'll become my best friend."

"Of course he will," cried Peter, eagerly sniffing at the red herring Lancelot had thrown across the track. "You stand out for a royalty on every copy, so that if you strike ile—oh, I beg your pardon, that's another of the phrases you object to, isn't it?"

"Don't be a fool," said Lancelot, laughing on. "You know I only object to that in connection with English peers marrying the daughters of men who have done it."

"Oh, is that it? I wish you'd publish an expurgated dictionary with most of the words left out, and exact definitions of the conditions under which one may use the remainder. But I've got on a siding. What was I talking about?"

"Royalty," muttered Lancelot languidly.

"Royalty? No. You mentioned the aristocracy, I think." Then he burst into a hearty laugh. "Oh yes—on that ballad. Now, look here! I've brought a ballad with me just to show you—a thing that is going like wildfire."

"'Not Good-night and good-bye, I hope," laughed Lancelot.

"Yes—the very one!" cried Peter, astonished.

"Himmel!" groaned Lancelot in comic despair.

"You know it already?" inquired Peter eagerly.

"No; only I can't open a paper without seeing the advertisement and the sickly-sentimental refrain."

"You see how famous it is, anyway," said Peter. "And if you want to strike—er—to make a hit you'll just take that song and do a deliberate imitation of it."

"Wha-a-a-t!" gasped Lancelot.

"My dear chap, they all do it. When the public cotton to a thing they can't have enough of it."

"But I can write my own rot, surely."

"In the face of all this litter of 'Ops.' I daren't dispute that for a moment. But it isn't enough to write rot—the public want a particular kind of rot. Now just play that over—oblige me." He laid both hands on Lancelot's shoulders in amicable appeal.

Lancelot shrugged them, but seated himself at the piano, played the introductory chords, and commenced singing the words in his pleasant baritone.

Suddenly Beethoven ran towards the door, howling.

Lancelot ceased playing and looked approvingly at the animal.

"By Jove! He wants to go out. What an ear for music that animal's got!"

Peter smiled grimly. "It's long enough. I suppose that's why you call him Beethoven."

"Not at all. Beethoven had no ear—at least not in his latest period—he was deaf. Lucky devil! That is, if this sort of thing was brought round on barrel-organs."

"Never mind, old man! Finish the thing."

"But consider Beethoven's feelings!"

"Hang Beethoven!"

"Poor Beethoven. Come here, my poor maligned musical critic! Would they give you a bad name and hang you? Now you must be very quiet. Put your paws into those lovely long ears of yours if it gets too horrible. You have been used to high-class music, I know, but this is the sort of thing that England expects every man to do, so the sooner you get used to it the better." He ran his fingers along the keys. "There, Peter, he's growling already. I'm sure he'll start again, the moment I strike the theme."

"Let him! We'll take it as a spaniel obligato."

"Oh, but his accompaniments are too staccato. He has no sense of time."

"Why don't you teach him, then, to wag his tail like the pendulum of a metronome? He'd be more use to you that way than setting up to be a musician, which Nature never meant him for—his hair's not long enough. But go ahead, old man, Beethoven's behaving himself now."

Indeed, as if he were satisfied with his protest, the little beast remained quiet, while his lord and master went through the piece. He did not even interrupt at the refrain.

"Kiss me, good-night, dear love,   Dream of the old delight;   My spirit is summoned above,   Kiss me, dear love, good-night."

"I must say it's not so awful as I expected," said Lancelot candidly; "it's not at all bad—for a waltz."

"There, you see!" said Peter eagerly; "the public are not such fools after all."

"Still, the words are the most maudlin twaddle!" said Lancelot, as if he found some consolation in the fact.

"Yes, but I didn't write them!" replied Peter quickly. Then he grew red and laughed an embarrassed laugh. "I didn't mean to tell you, old man. But there—the cat's out. That's what took me to Brahmson's that afternoon we met! And I harmonised it myself, mind you, every crotchet. I picked up enough at the Conservatoire for that. You know lots of fellows only do the tune—they give out all the other work."

"So you are the great Keeley Lesterre, eh?" said Lancelot in amused astonishment.

"Yes; I have to do it under another name. I don't want to grieve the old man. You see, I promised him to reform, when he took me back to his heart and business."

"Is that strictly honouraole, Peter?" said Lancelot, shaking his head.

"Oh well! I couldn't give it up altogether, but I do practically stick to the contract—it's all overtime, you know. It doesn't interfere a bit with business. Besides, as you'd say, it isn't music," he said slyly. "And just because I don't want it I make a heap of coin out of it—that's why I'm so vexed at your keeping me still in your debt."

Lancelot frowned. "Then you had no difficulty in getting published?" he asked.

"I don't say that. It was bribery and corruption so far as my first song was concerned. I tipped a professional to go down and tell Brahmson he was going to take it up. You know, of course, well-known singers get half a guinea from the publisher every time they sing a song."

"No; do they?" said Lancelot. "How mean of them."

"Business, my boy. It pays the publisher to give it them. Look at the advertisement!"

"But suppose a really fine song was published and the publisher refused to pay this blood-money?"

"Then I suppose they'd sing some other song, and let that moulder on the foolish publisher's shelves."

"Great heavens!" said Lancelot, jumping up from the piano in wild excitement. "Then a musician's reputation is really at the mercy of a mercenary crew of singers, who respect neither art nor themselves. Oh yes, we are indeed a musical people!"

"Easy there! Several of 'em are pals of mine, and I'll get them to take up those ballads of yours as soon as you write 'em."

"Let them go to the devil with their ballads!" roared Lancelot, and with a sweep of his arm whirled Good-night and good-bye into the air. Peter picked it up and wrote something on it with a stylographic pen which he produced from his waistcoat pocket.

"There!" he said, "that'll make you remember it's your own property—and mine—that you are treating so disrespectfully."

"I beg your pardon, old chap," said Lancelot, rebuked and remorseful.

"Don't mention it," replied Peter. "And whenever you decide to become rich and famous—there's your model."

"Never! never! never!' cried Lancelot, when Peter went at ten. "My poor Beethoven! What you must have suffered! Never mind, I'll play you your Moonlight sonata."

He touched the keys gently, and his sorrows and his temptations faded from him. He glided into Bach, and then into Chopin and Mendelssohn, and at last drifted into dreamy improvisation, his fingers moving almost of themselves, his eyes, half closed, seeing only inward visions.

And then, all at once, he awoke with a start, for Beethoven was barking towards the door, with pricked-up ears and rigid tail.

"Sh! You little beggar," he murmured, becoming conscious that the hour was late, and that he himself had been noisy at unbeseeming hours. "What's the matter with you?" And, with a sudden thought, he threw open the door.

It was merely Mary Ann.

Her face—flashed so unexpectedly upon him—had the piquancy of a vision, but its expression was one of confusion and guilt; there were tears on her cheeks; in her hand was a bed-room candlestick.

She turned quickly, and began to mount the stairs. Lancelot put his hand on her shoulder, and turned her face towards him, and said in an imperious whisper:

"Now then, what's up? What are you crying about?"

"I ain't—I mean I'm not crying," said Mary Ann, with a sob in her breath.

"Come, come, don't fib. What's the matter?"

"I'm not crying; it's only the music," she murmured.

"The music," he echoed, bewildered.

"Yessir. The music always makes me cry—but you can't call it crying—it feels so nice."

"Oh, then you've been listening!"

"Yessir." Her eyes drooped in humiliation.

"But you ought to have been in bed," he said. "You get little enough sleep as it is."

"It's better than sleep," she answered.

The simple phrase vibrated through him like a beautiful minor chord. He smoothed her hair tenderly.

"Poor child!" he said.

There was an instant's silence. It was past midnight, and the house was painfully still. They stood upon the dusky landing, across which a bar of light streamed from his half-open door, and only Beethoven's eyes were upon them. But Lancelot felt no impulse to fondle her; only just to lay his hand on her hair, as in benediction and pity.

"So you liked what I was playing," he said, not without a pang of personal pleasure.

"Yessir; I never heard you play that before."

"So you often listen!"

"I can hear you, even in the kitchen. Oh, it's just lovely! I don't care what I have to do then, if it's grates or plates or steps. The music goes and goes, and I feel back in the country again, and standing, as I used to love to stand of an evening, by the stile, under the big elm, and watch how the sunset did redden the white birches, and fade in the water. Oh, it was so nice in the springtime, with the hawthorn that grew on the other bank, and the bluebells—"

The pretty face was full of dreamy tenderness, the eyes lit up witchingly. She pulled herself up suddenly, and stole a shy glance at her auditor.

"Yes, yes, go on," he said; "tell me all you feel about the music."

"And there's one song you sometimes play that makes me feel floating on and on like a great white swan."

She hummed a few bars of the Gondel-Lied—flawlessly.

"Dear me! you have an ear!" he said, pinching it. "And how did you like what I was playing just now?" he went on, growing curious to know how his own improvisations struck her.

"Oh, I liked it so much," she whispered enthusiastically, "because it reminded me of my favourite one— every moment I did think—I thought—you were going to come into that."

The whimsical sparkle leapt into his eyes.

"And I thought I was so original," he murmured.

"But what I liked best," she began, then checked herself, as if suddenly remembering she had never made a spontaneous remark before, and lacking courage to establish a precedent.

"Yes—what you liked best?" he said encouragingly.

"That song you sang this afternoon," she said shyly.

"What song? I sang no song," he said, puzzled for a moment.

"Oh yes! That one about—

'Kiss me, dear love, good-night.'

I was going upstairs, but it made me stop just here—and cry."

He made his comic grimace.

"So it was you Beethoven was barking at! And I thought he had an ear! And I thought you had an ear! But no! You're both Philistines, after all. Heigho!"

She looked sad. "Oughtn't I to ha' liked it?" she asked anxiously.

"Oh yes," he said reassuringly, "it's very popular. No drawing-room is without it."

She detected the ironic ring in his voice. "It wasn't so much the music," she began apologetically.

"Now—now you're going to spoil yourself," he said. "Be natural."

"But it wasn't," she protested. "It was the words—"

"That's worse," he murmured below his breath.

"They reminded me of my mother as she laid dying."

"Ah!" said Lancelot.

"Yes, sir, mother was a long time dying—it was when I was a little girl, and I used to nurse her—I fancy it was our little Sally's death that killed her; she took to her bed after the funeral, and never left it till she went to her own," said Mary Ann, with unconscious flippancy. "She used to look up to the ceiling and say that she was going to little Sally, and I remember I was such a silly then, I brought mother flowers and apples and bits of cake to take to Sally with my love. I put them on her pillow, but the flowers faded and the cake got mouldy—mother was such a long time dying—and at last I ate the apples myself, I was so tired of waiting. Wasn't I silly?" And Mary Ann laughed a little laugh with tears in it. Then growing grave again, she added: "And at last, when mother was really on the point of death, she forgot all about little Sally, and said she was going to meet Tom. And I remember thinking she was going to America. I didn't know people talk nonsense before they die."

"They do—a great deal of it, unfortunately," said Lancelot lightly, trying to disguise from himself that his eyes were moist. He seemed to realise now what she was—a child; a child who, simpler than most children to start with, had grown only in body, whose soul had been stunted by uncounted years of dull and monotonous drudgery. The blood burnt in his veins as he thought of the cruelty of circumstance and the heartless honesty of her mistress. He made up his mind for the second time to give Mrs. Leadbatter a piece of his mind in the morning.

"Well, go to bed now, my poor child," he said, "or you'll get no rest at all."

"Yessir."

She went obediently up a couple of stairs, then turned her head appealingly towards him. The tears still glimmered on her eyelashes. For an instant he thought she was expecting her kiss, but she only wanted to explain anxiously once again, "That was why I liked that song, 'Kiss me, good-night, dear love.' It was what my mother—"

"Yes, yes, I understand," he broke in, half amused, though somehow the words did not seem so full of maudlin pathos to him now. "And there—"—he drew her head towards him—"Kiss me, good-night—"

He did not complete the quotation; indeed, her lips were already drawn too close to his. But, ere he released her, the long-repressed thought had found expression.

"You don't kiss anybody but me?" he said half playfully.

"Oh no, sir," said Mary Ann earnestly.

"What!" more lightly still. "Haven't you got half a dozen young men?"

Mary Ann shook her head, more regretfully than resentfully. "I told you I never go out—except for little errands."

She had told him, but his attention had been so concentrated on the ungrammatical form in which she had conveyed the information, that the fact itself had made no impression. Now his anger against Mrs. Leadbatter dwindled. After all, she was wise in not giving Mary Ann the run of the London streets.

"But"—he hesitated. "How about the—the milkman—and the—the other gentlemen."

"Please, sir," said Mary Ann, "I don't like them."

After that no man could help expressing his sense of her good taste.

"Then you won't kiss anybody but me," he said, as he let her go for the last time. He had a Quixotic sub-consciousness that he was saving her from his kind by making her promise formally.

"How could I, Mr. Lancelot?" And the brimming eyes shone with soft light. "I never shall—never."

It sounded like a troth.

He went back to the room and shut the door, but could not shut out her image. The picture she had unwittingly supplied of herself took possession of his imagination: he saw her almost as a dream-figure—the virginal figure he knew—standing by the stream in the sunset, amid the elms and silver birches, with daisies in her hands and bluebells at her feet, inhaling the delicate scent that wafted from the white hawthorn bushes, and watching the water glide along till it seemed gradually to wash away the fading colours of the sunset that glorified it. And as he dwelt on the vision he felt harmonies and phrases stirring and singing in his brain, like a choir of awakened birds. Quickly he seized paper and wrote down the theme that flowed out at the point of his pen—a reverie full of the haunting magic of quiet waters and woodland sunsets and the gracious innocence of maidenhood. When it was done he felt he must give it a distinctive name. He cast about for one, pondering and rejecting titles innumerable. Countless lines of poetry ran through his head, from which he sought to pick a word or two as one plucks a violet from a posy. At last a half-tender, half-whimsical look came into his face, and picking his pen out of his hair, he wrote merely—"Marianne."

It was only natural that Mary Ann should be unable to maintain herself—or be maintained—at this idyllic level. But her fall was aggravated by two circumstances, neither of which had any particular business to occur. The first was an intimation from the misogamist German Professor that he had persuaded another of his old pupils to include a prize symphony by Lancelot in the programme of a Crystal Palace Concert. This was of itself sufficient to turn Lancelot's head away from all but thoughts of Fame, even if Mary Ann had not been luckless enough to be again discovered cleaning the steps—and without gloves. Against such a spectacle the veriest idealist is powerless. If Mary Ann did not immediately revert to the category of quadrupeds in which she had started, it was only because of Lancelot's supplementary knowledge of the creature. But as he passed her by, solicitous as before not to tread upon her, he felt as if all the cold water in her pail were pouring down the back of his neck.

Nevertheless, the effect of both these turns of fortune was transient. The symphony was duly performed, and dismissed in the papers as promising, if over-ambitious; the only tangible result was a suggestion from the popular composer, who was a member of his club, that Lancelot should collaborate with him in a comic opera, for the production of which he had facilities. The composer confessed he had a fluent gift of tune, but had no liking for the drudgery of orchestration, and as Lancelot was well up in these tedious technicalities, the two might strike a partnership to mutual advantage.

Lancelot felt insulted, but retained enough mastery of himself to reply that he would think it over. As he gave no signs of life or thought, the popular composer then wrote to him at length on the subject, offering him fifty pounds for the job, half of it on account. Lancelot was in sore straits when he got the letter, for his stock of money was dwindling to vanishing point, and he dallied with the temptation sufficiently to take the letter home with him. But his spirit was not yet broken, and the letter, crumpled like a rag, was picked up by Mary Ann and straightened out, and carefully placed upon the mantel-shelf.

Time did something of a similar service for Mary Ann herself, picking her up from the crumpled attitude in which Lancelot had detected her on the doorstep, straightening her out again, and replacing her upon her semi-poetic pedestal. But, as with the cream-laid notepaper, the wrinklings could not be effaced entirely; which was more serious for Mary Ann.

Not that Mary Ann was conscious of these diverse humours in Lancelot. Unconscious of changes in herself, she could not conceive herself related to his variations of mood; still less did she realise the inward struggle of which she was the cause. She was vaguely aware that he had external worries, for all his grandeur, and if he was by turns brusque, affectionate, indifferent, playful, brutal, charming, callous, demonstrative, she no more connected herself with these vicissitudes than with the caprices of the weather. If her sun smiled once a day it was enough. How should she know that his indifference was often a victory over himself, as his amativeness was a defeat?

If any excuse could be found for Lancelot, it would be that which he administered to his conscience morning and evening like a soothing syrup. His position was grown so desperate that Mary Ann almost stood between him and suicide. Continued disappointment made his soul sick; his proud heart fed on itself. He would bite his lips till the blood came, vowing never to give in. And not only would he not move an inch from his ideal, he would rather die than gratify Peter by falling back on him; he would never even accept that cheque which was virtually his own.

It was wonderful how, in his stoniest moments, the sight of Mary Ann's candid face, eloquent with dumb devotion, softened and melted him. He would take her gloved hand and press it silently. And Mary Ann never knew one iota of his inmost thought! He could not bring himself to that; indeed, she never for a moment appeared to him in the light of an intelligent being; at her best she was a sweet, simple, loving child. And he scarce spoke to her at all now—theirs was a silent communion—he had no heart to converse with her as he had done. The piano, too, was almost silent; the canary sang less and less, though spring was coming, and glints of sunshine stole between the wires of its cage; even Beethoven sometimes failed to bark when there was a knock at the street door.

And at last there came a day when—for the first time in his life—Lancelot inspected his wardrobe, and hunted together his odds and ends of jewelry. From this significant task he was aroused by hearing Mrs. Leadbatter coughing in his sitting-room.

He went in with an interrogative look.

"Oh, my chest!" said Mrs. Leadbatter, patting it. "It's no use my denyin' of it, sir, I'm done up. It's as much as I can do to crawl up to the top to bed. I'm thinkin' I shall have to make up a bed in the kitchen. It only shows 'ow right I was to send for my Rosie, though quite the lady, and where will you find a nattier nursemaid in al Bayswater?"

"Nowhere," assented Lancelot automatically.

"Oh, I didn't know you'd noticed her running in to see 'er pore old mother of a Sunday arternoon," said Mrs. Leadbatter, highly gratified. "Well, sir, I won't say anything about the hextry gas, though a poor widder and sevenpence hextry on the thousand, but I'm thinkin' if you would give my Rosie a lesson once a week on that there pianner, it would be a kind of set-off, for you know, sir, the policeman tells me your winder is a landmark to 'im on the foggiest nights."

Lancelot flushed, then wrinkled his brows. This was a new idea altogether. Mrs. Leadbatter stood waiting for his reply, with a deferential smile tempered by asthmatic contortions.

"But have you got a piano of your own?"

"Oh no, sir," cried Mrs. Leadbatter almost reproachfully.

"Well; but how is your Rosie to practise? One lesson a week is of very little use anyway, but unless she practises a good deal it'll only be a waste of time."

"Ah, you don't know my Rosie," said Mrs. Leadbatter, shaking her head with sceptical pride. "You mustn't judge by other gels—the way that gel picks up things is—well, I'll just tell you what 'er school-teacher, Miss Whiteman, said. She says—"

"My good lady," interrupted Lancelot, "I practised six hours a day myself."

"Yes, but it don't come so natural to a man," said Mrs. Leadbatter, unshaken. "And it don't look natural neither to see a man playin' the pianner—it's like seein' him knittin'."

But Lancelot was knitting his brows in a way that was exceedingly natural. "I may as well tell you at once that what you propose is impossible. First of all, because I am doubtful whether I shall remain in these rooms; and secondly, because I am giving up the piano immediately. I only have it on hire, and I—I—" He felt himself blushing.

"Oh, what a pity!" interrupted Mrs. Leadbatter. "You might as well let me go on payin' the hinstalments, instead of lettin' all you've paid go for nothing. Rosie ain't got much time, but I could allow 'er a 'our a day if it was my own pianner."

Lancelot explained "hire" did not mean the "hire system." But the idea of acquiring the piano having once fired Mrs. Leadbatter's brain, could not be extinguished. The unexpected conclusion arrived at was that she was to purchase the piano on the hire system, allowing it to stand in Lancelot's room, and that five shillings a week should be taken off his rent in return for six lessons of an hour each, one of the hours counterbalancing the gas grievance. Reviewing the bargain, when Mrs. Leadbatter was gone, Lancelot did not think it at all bad for him. "Use of the piano. Gas," he murmured, with a pathetic smile, recalling the advertisements he had read before lighting on Mrs. Leadbatter's. "And five shillings a week—it's a considerable relief! There's no loss of dignity either—for nobody will know. But I wonder what the governor would have said!"

The thought shook him with silent laughter; a spectator might have fancied he was sobbing.

But, after the lessons began, it might almost be said it was only when a spectator was present that he was not sobbing. For Rosie, who was an awkward, ungraceful young person, proved to be the dullest and most butter-fingered pupil ever invented for the torture of teachers; at least, so Lancelot thought, but then he had never had any other pupils, and was not patient. It must be admitted, though, that Rosie giggled perpetually, apparently finding endless humour in her own mistakes. But the climax of the horror was the attendance of Mrs. Leadbatter at the lessons, for, to Lancelot's consternation, she took it for granted that her presence was part of the contract. She marched into the room in her best cap, and sat, smiling, in the easy-chair, wheezing complacently and beating time with her foot. Occasionally she would supplement Lancelot's critical observations.

"It ain't as I fears to trust 'er with you, sir," she also remarked about three times a week, "for I knows, sir, you're a gentleman. But it's the neighbours; they never can mind their own business. I told 'em you was going to give my Rosie lessons, and you know, sir, that they will talk of what don't concern 'em. And, after all, sir, it's an hour, and an hour is sixty minutes, ain't it, sir?"

And Lancelot, groaning inwardly, and unable to deny this chronometry, felt that an ironic Providence was punishing him for his attentions to Mary Ann.

And yet he only felt more tenderly towards Mary Ann. Contrasted with these two vulgar females, whom he came to conceive as her oppressors, sitting in gauds and finery, and taking lessons which had better befitted their Cinderella—the figure of Mary Ann definitely reassumed some of its antediluvian poetry, if we may apply the adjective to that catastrophic washing of the steps. And Mary Ann herself had grown gloomier—once or twice he thought she had been crying, though he was too numbed and apathetic to ask, and was incapable of suspecting that Rosie had anything to do with her tears. He hardly noticed that Rosie had taken to feeding the canary; the question of how he should feed himself was becoming every day more and more menacing. He saw starvation slowly closing in upon him like the walls of a torture-chamber. He had grown quite familiar with the pawnshop now, though he still slipped in as though his goods were stolen.

And at last there came a moment when Lancelot felt he could bear it no longer. And then he suddenly saw daylight. Why should he teach only Rosie? Nay, why should he teach Rosie at all? If he was reduced to giving lessons—and after all it was no degradation to do so, no abandonment of his artistic ideal, rather a solution of the difficulty so simple that he wondered it had not occurred to him before—why should he give them at so wretched a price? He would get another pupil, other pupils, who would enable him to dispense with the few shillings he made by Rosie. He would not ask anybody to recommend him pupils—there was no need for his acquaintances to know, and if he asked Peter, Peter would probably play him some philanthropic trick. No, he would advertise.

After he had spent his last gold breast-pin in advertisements, he realised that to get piano-forte pupils in London was as easy as to get songs published. By the time he had quite realised it, it was May, and then he sat down to realise his future.

The future was sublimely simple—as simple as his wardrobe had grown. All his clothes were on his back. In a week or two he would be on the streets; for a poor widow could not be expected to lodge, partially board (with use of the piano, gas), an absolutely penniless young gentleman, though he combined the blood of twenty county families with the genius of a pleiad of tone-poets.

There was only one bright spot in the prospect. Rosie's lessons would come to an end.

What he would do when he got on the streets was not so clear as the rest of this prophetic vision. He might take to a barrel-organ—but that would be a cruel waste of his artistic touch. Perhaps he would die on a doorstep, like the professor of many languages whose starvation was recorded in that very morning's paper.

Thus, driven by the saturnine necessity that sneers at our puny resolutions, Lancelot began to meditate surrender. For surrender of some sort must be—either of life or ideal. After so steadfast and protracted a struggle—oh, it was cruel, it was terrible; how noble, how high-minded he had been; and this was how the fates dealt with him—but at that moment—

"Sw—eêt" went the canary, and filled the room with its rapturous demi-semi-quavers, its throat swelling, its little body throbbing with joy of the sunshine. And then Lancelot remembered—not the joy of the sunshine, not the joy of life—no, merely Mary Ann.

Noble! high-minded! No, let Peter think that, let posterity think that. But he could not cozen himself thus! He had fallen—horribly, vulgarly. How absurd of him to set himself up as a saint, a martyr, an idealist! He could not divide himself into two compartments like that and pretend that only one counted in his character. Who was he, to talk of dying for art? No, he was but an everyday man. He wanted Mary Ann—yes, he might as well admit that to himself now. It was no use hum-bugging himself any longer. Why should he give her up? She was his discovery, his treasure-trove, his property.

And if he could stoop to her, why should he not stoop to popular work, to devilling, to anything that would rid him of these sordid cares? Bah! away with all pretences?

Was not this shamefaced pawning as vulgar, as wounding to the artist's soul, as the turning out of tawdry melodies?

Yes, he would escape from Mrs. Leadbatter and her Rosie; he would write to that popular composer—he had noticed his letter lying on the mantel-piece the other day—and accept the fifty pounds, and whatever he did he could do anonymously, so that Peter wouldn't know, after all; he would escape from this wretched den and take a flat far away, somewhere where nobody knew him, and there he would sit and work, with Mary Ann for his housekeeper. Poor Mary Ann! How glad she would be when he told her! The tears came into his eyes as he thought of her naïve delight. He would rescue her from this horrid, monotonous slavery, and—happy thought—he would have her to give lessons to instead of Rosie.

Yes, he would refine her; prune away all that reminded him of her wild growth, so that it might no longer humiliate him to think to what a companion he had sunk. How happy they would be! Of course the world would censure him if it knew, but the world was stupid and prosaic, and measured all things by its coarse rule of thumb. It was the best thing that could happen to Mary Ann—the best thing in the world. And then the world wouldn't know.

"Sw—eêt," went the canary. "Sw—eêt."

This time the joy of the bird penetrated to his own soul—the joy of life, the joy of the sunshine. He rang the bell violently, as though he were sounding a clarion of defiance, the trumpet of youth.

Mary Ann knocked at the door, came in, and began to draw on her gloves.

He was in a mad mood—the incongruity struck him so that he burst out into a roar of laughter.

Mary Ann paused, flushed, and bit her lip. The touch of resentment he had never noted before gave her a novel charm, spicing her simplicity.

He came over to her and took her half-bare hands. No, they were not so terrible, after all. Perhaps she had awakened to her iniquities, and had been trying to wash them white. His last hesitation as to her worthiness to live with him vanished.

"Mary Ann," he said, "I'm going to leave these rooms."

The flush deepened, but the anger faded. She was a child again—her big eyes full of tears. He felt her hands tremble in his.

"Mary Ann," he went on, "how would you like me to take you with me?"

"Do you mean it, sir?" she asked eagerly.

"Yes, dear." It was the first time he had used the word. The blood throbbed madly in her ears. "If you will come with me—and be my little housekeeper—we will go away to some nice spot, and be quite alone together—in the country if you like, amid the foxglove and the meadowsweet, or by the green waters, where you shall stand in the sunset and dream; and I will teach you music and the piano"—her eyes dilated—"and you shall not do any of this wretched nasty work any more. What do you say?"

"Sw—eêt, sw—eêt," said the canary in thrilling jubilation.

Her happiness was choking her—she could not speak.

"And we will take the canary, too—unless I say good-bye to you as well."

"Oh no, you mustn't leave us here!"

"And then," he said slowly, "it will not be good-bye—nor good-night. Do you understand?"

"Yes, yes," she breathed, and her face shone.

"But think, think, Mary Ann," he said, a sudden pang of compunction shooting through his breast. He released her hands. "Do you understand?"

"I understand—I shall be with you, always."

He replied uneasily: "I shall look after you—always."

"Yes, yes," she breathed. Her bosom heaved. "Always."

Then his very first impression of her as "a sort of white Topsy" recurred to him suddenly and flashed into speech.

"Mary Ann, I don't believe you know how you came into the world. I dare say you 'specs you growed.'"

"No, sir," said Mary Ann gravely; "God made me."

That shook him strangely for a moment. But the canary sang on:

"Sw-eêt. Sw-w-w-w-w-eêt."

III

And so it was settled. He wrote the long-delayed answer to the popular composer, found him still willing to give out his orchestration, and they met by appointment at the club.

"I've got hold of a splendid book," said the popular composer. "Awfully clever; jolly original. Bound to go—from the French, you know. Haven't had time to set to work on it—old engagement to run over to Monte Carlo for a few days—but I'll leave you the book; you might care to look over it. And—I say—if any catchy tunes suggest themselves as you go along, you might just jot them down, you know. Not worth while losing an idea; eh, my boy! Ha! ha! ha! Well, good-bye. See you again when I come back; don't suppose I shall be away more than a month. Good-bye!" And, having shaken Lancelot's hand with tremendous cordiality, the popular composer rushed downstairs and into a hansom.

Lancelot walked home with the libretto and the five five-pound notes. He asked for Mrs. Leadbatter, and gave her a week's notice. He wanted to drop Rosie immediately, on the plea of pressure of work, but her mother received the suggestion with ill-grace, and said that Rosie should come up and practise on her own piano all the same, so he yielded to the complexities of the situation, and found hope a wonderful sweetener of suffering. Despite Rosie and her giggling, and Mrs. Leadbatter and her best cap and her asthma, the week went by almost cheerfully. He worked regularly at the comic opera, nearly as happy as the canary which sang all day long, and, though scarcely a word more passed between him and Mary Ann, their eyes met ever and anon in the consciousness of a sweet secret.

It was already Friday afternoon. He gathered together his few personal belongings—his books, his manuscripts, opera innumerable. There was room in his portmanteau for everything—now he had no clothes. On the Monday the long nightmare would be over. He would go down to some obscure seaside nook and live very quietly for a few weeks, and gain strength and calm in the soft spring airs, and watch hand-in-hand with Mary Ann the rippling scarlet trail of the setting sun fade across the green waters. Life, no doubt, would be hard enough still. Struggles and trials enough were yet before him, but he would not think of that now—enough that for a month or two there would be bread and cheese and kisses. And then, in the midst of a tender reverie, with his hand on the lid of his portmanteau, he was awakened by ominous sounds of objurgation from the kitchen.

His heart stood still. He went down a few stairs and listened.

"Not another stroke of work do you do in my house, Mary Ann!" Then there was silence, save for the thumping of his own heart. What had happened?

He heard Mrs. Leadbatter mounting the kitchen stairs, wheezing and grumbling: "Well, of all the sly little things!"

Mary Ann had been discovered. His blood ran cold at the thought. The silly creature had been unable to keep the secret.

"Not a word about 'im all this time. Oh, the sly little thing. Who would hever a-believed it?"

And then, in the intervals of Mrs. Leadbatter's groanings, there came to him the unmistakable sound of Mary Ann sobbing—violently, hysterically. He turned from cold to hot in a fever of shame and humiliation. How had it all come about? Oh yes, he could guess. The gloves! What a fool he had been! Mrs. Leadbatter had unearthed the box. Why did he give her more than the pair that could always be kept hidden in her pocket? Yes, it was the gloves. And then there was the canary. Mrs. Leadbatter had suspected he was leaving her for a reason. She had put two and two together, she had questioned Mary Ann, and the ingenuous little idiot had naïvely told her he was going to take her with him. It didn't really matter, of course; he didn't suppose Mrs. Leadbatter could exercise any control over Mary Ann, but it was horrible to be discussed by her and Rosie; and then there was that meddlesome vicar, who might step in and make things nasty.

Mrs. Leadbatter's steps and wheezes and grumblings had arrived in the passage, and Lancelot hastily stole back into his room, his heart continuing to flutter painfully.

He heard the complex noises reach his landing, pass by, and move up higher. She wasn't coming in to him, then. He could endure the suspense no longer; he threw open his door and said, "Is there anything the matter?"

Mrs. Leadbatter paused and turned her head.

"His there anything the matter!" she echoed, looking down upon him. "A nice thing when a woman's troubled with hastmer, and brought 'ome 'er daughter to take 'er place, that she should 'ave to start 'untin' afresh!"

"Why, is Rosie going away?" he said, immeasurably relieved.

"My Rosie! She's the best girl breathing. It's that there Mary Ann!"

"Wh-a-t!" he stammered. "Mary Ann leaving you?"

"Well, you don't suppose," replied Mrs. Leadbatter angrily, "as I can keep a gel in my kitchen as is a-goin' to 'ave 'er own nors-end-kerridge!"

"Her own horse and carriage!" repeated Lancelot, utterly dazed. "What ever are you talking about?"

"Well—there's the letter!" exclaimed Mrs. Leadbatter indignantly. "See for yourself if you don't believe me. I don't know how much two and a 'arf million dollars is—but it sounds unkimmonly like a nors-end-kerridge—and never said a word about 'im the whole time, the sly little thing!"

The universe seemed oscillating so that he grasped at the letter like a drunken man. It was from the vicar. He wrote:

"I have much pleasure in informing you that our dear Mary Ann is the fortunate inheritress of two and a half million dollars by the death of her brother Tom, who, as I learn from the lawyers who have applied to me for news of the family, has just died in America, leaving his money to his surviving relatives. He was rather a wild young man, but it seems he became the lucky possessor of some petroleum wells, which made him wealthy in a few months. I pray God Mary Ann may make a better use of the money than he would have done, I want you to break the news to her, please, and to prepare her for my visit. As I have to preach on Sunday, I cannot come to town before, but on Monday (D.V.) I shall run up and shall probably take her back with me, as I desire to help her through the difficulties that will attend her entry into the new life. How pleased you will be to think of the care you took of the dear child during these last five years. I hope she is well and happy. I think you omitted to write to me last Christmas on the subject. Please give her my kindest regards and best wishes, and say I shall be with her (D.V.) on Monday."

The words swam uncertainly before Lancelot's eyes, but he got through them all at last. He felt chilled and numbed. He averted his face as he handed the letter back to Mary Ann's "missus."

"What a fortunate girl!" he said in a low, stony voice.

"Fortunate ain't the word for it. The mean, sly little cat. Fancy never telling me a word about 'er brother all these years—me as 'as fed her, and clothed her, and lodged her, and kepper out of all mischief, as if she'd bin my own daughter, never let her go out Bankhollidayin' in loose company—as you can bear witness yourself, sir—and eddicated 'er out of 'er country talk and rough ways, and made 'er the smart young woman she is, fit to wait on the most troublesome of gentlemen. And now she'll go away and say I used 'er 'arsh, and overworked 'er, and Lord knows what, don't tell me. Oh, my poor chest!"

"I think you may make your mind quite easy," said Lancelot grimly. "I'm sure Mary Ann is perfectly satisfied with your treatment."

"But she ain't—there, listen! don't you hear her going on?" Poor Mary Ann's sobs were still audible, though exhaustion was making them momently weaker. "She's been going on like that ever since I broke the news to 'er and gave her a piece of my mind—the sly little cat! She wanted to go on scrubbing the kitchen, and I had to take the brush away by main force. A nice thing, indeed! A gel as can keep a nors-end-kerridge down on the cold kitchen stones! 'Twasn't likely I could allow that. 'No, Mary Ann,' says I firmly, 'you're a lady, and if you don't know what's proper for a lady, you'd best listen to them as does. You go and buy yourself a dress and a jacket to be ready for that vicar, who's been a real good kind friend to you. He's coming to take you away on Monday, he is, and how will you look in that dirty print? Here's a suvrin,' says I, 'out of my 'ard-earned savin's—and get a pair o' boots, too; you can git a sweet pair for 2s. 11d. at Rackstraw's afore the sale closes,' and with that I shoves the suvrin into 'er hand instead o' the scrubbin' brush, and what does she do? Why, busts out a-cryin', and sits on the damp stones, and sobs, and sulks, and stares at the suvrin in her hand as if I'd told her of a funeral instead of a fortune!" concluded Mrs. Leadbatter alliteratively.

"But you did—her brother's death," said Lancelot. "That's what she's crying about."

Mrs. Leadbatter was taken aback by this obverse view of the situation; but, recovering herself, she shook her head. "I wouldn't cry for no brother that lef me to starve when he was rollin' in two and a 'arf million dollars," she said sceptically. "And I'm sure my Rosie wouldn't. But she never 'ad nobody to leave her money, poor dear child, except me, please Gaud. It's only the fools as 'as the luck in this world." And having thus relieved her bosom, she resumed her panting progress upwards.

The last words rang on in Lancelot's ears long after he had returned to his room. In the utter breakdown and confusion of his plans and his ideas it was the one definite thought he clung to, as a swimmer in a whirlpool clings to a rock. His brain refused to concentrate itself on any other aspect of the situation—he could not, would not, dared not, think of anything else. He knew vaguely he ought to rejoice with her over her wonderful stroke of luck, that savoured of the fairy-story, but everything was swamped by that one almost resentful reflection. Oh, the irony of fate! Blind fate showering torrents of gold upon this foolish, babyish household drudge, who was all emotion and animal devotion, without the intellectual outlook of a Hottentot, and leaving men of genius to starve, or sell their souls for a handful of it! How was the wisdom of the ages justified! Verily did fortune favour fools. And Tom—the wicked—he had flourished as the wicked always do, like the green bay tree, as the Psalmist discovered ever so many centuries ago.

But gradually the wave of bitterness waned. He found himself listening placidly and attentively to the joyous trills and roulades of the canary, till the light faded and the grey dusk crept into the room and stilled the tiny winged lover of the sunshine. Then Beethoven came and rubbed himself against his master's leg, and Lancelot got up as one wakes from a dream, and stretched his cramped limbs dazedly, and rang the bell mechanically for tea. He was groping on the mantel-piece for the matches when the knock at the door came, and he did not turn round till he had found them. He struck a light, expecting to see Mrs. Leadbatter or Rosie. He started to find it was merely Mary Ann.

But she was no longer merely Mary Ann, he remembered with another shock. She loomed large to him in the match-light—he seemed to see her through a golden haze. Tumultuous images of her glorified gilded future rose and mingled dizzily in his brain.

And yet, was he dreaming? Surely it was the same Mary Ann, with the same winsome face and the same large pathetic eyes, ringed though they were with the shadow of tears. Mary Ann, in her neat white cap—yes—and in her tan kid gloves. He rubbed his eyes. Was he really awake? Or—a thought still more dizzying—had he been dreaming? Had he fallen asleep and reinless fancy had played him the fantastic trick, from which, cramped and dazed, he had just awakened to the old sweet reality.

"Mary Ann," he cried wildly. The lighted match fell from his fingers and burnt itself out unheeded on the carpet.

"Yessir."

"Is it true"—his emotion choked him—"is it true you've come into two and a half million dollars?"

"Yessir, and I've brought you some tea."

The room was dark, but darkness seemed to fall on it as she spoke.

"But why are you waiting on me, then?" he said slowly. "Don't you know that you—that you—"

"Please, Mr. Lancelot, I wanted to come in and see you." He felt himself trembling.

"But Mrs. Leadbatter told me she wouldn't let you do any more work."

"I told missus that I must; I told her she couldn't get another girl before Monday, if then, and if she didn't let me I wouldn't buy a new dress and a pair of boots with her sovereign—it isn't suvrin, is it, sir?"

"No," murmured Lancelot, smiling in spite of himself.

"With her sovereign. And I said I would be all dirty on Monday."

"But what can you get for a sovereign?" he asked irrelevantly. He felt his mind wandering away from him.

"Oh, ever such a pretty cress!"

The picture of Mary Ann in a pretty dress painted itself upon the darkness. How lovely the child would look in some creamy white evening dress with a rose in her hair. He wondered that in all his thoughts of their future he had never dressed her up thus in fancy, to feast his eyes on the vision.

"And so the vicar will find you in a pretty dress," he said at last.

"No, sir."

"But you promised Mrs. Leadbatter to—"

"I promised to buy a dress with her sovereign. But I shan't be here when the vicar comes. He can't come till the afternoon."

"Why, where will you be?" he said, his heart beginning to beat fast.

"With you," she replied, with a faint accent of surprise.

He steadied himself against the mantel-piece.

"But—" he began, and ended, "is that honest?"

He dimly descried her lips pouting. "We can always send her another when we have one," she said.

He stood there, dumb, glad of the darkness.

"I must go down now," she said. "I mustn't stay long."

"Why?" he articulated.

"Rosie," she replied briefly.

"What about Rosie?"

"She watches me—ever since she came. Don't you understand?"

This time he was the dullard. He felt an extra quiver of repugnance for Rosie, but said nothing, while Mary Ann briskly lit the gas and threw some coals on the decaying fire. He was pleased she was going down; he was suffocating; he did not know what to say to her. And yet, as she was disappearing through the doorway, he had a sudden feeling things couldn't be allowed to remain an instant in this impossible position.

"Mary Ann," he cried.

"Yessir."

She turned back—her face wore merely the expectant expression of a summoned servant. The childishness of her behaviour confused him, irritated him.

"Are you foolish?" he cried suddenly; half regretting the phrase the instant he had uttered it.

Her lip twitched.

"No, Mr. Lancelot!" she faltered.

"But you talk as if you were," he said less roughly. "You mustn't run away from the vicar just when he is going to take you to the lawyer's to certify who you are, and see that you get your money."

"But I don't want to go with the vicar—I want to go with you. You said you would take me with you." She was almost in tears now.

"Yes—but don't you—don't you understand that—that," he stammered; then, temporising, "But I can wait."

"Can't the vicar wait?" said Mary Ann. He had never known her show such initiative.

He saw that it was hopeless—that the money had made no more dint upon her consciousness than some vague dream, that her whole being was set towards the new life with him, and shrank in horror from the menace of the vicar's withdrawal of her in the opposite direction. If joy and redemption had not already lain in the one quarter, the advantages of the other might have been more palpably alluring. As it was, her consciousness was "full up" in the matter, so to speak. He saw that he must tell her plain and plump, startle her out of her simple confidence.

"Listen to me, Mary Ann."

"Yessir."

"You are a young woman—not a baby. Strive to grasp what I am going to tell you."

"Yessir," in a half-sob, that vibrated with the obstinate resentment of a child that knows it is to be argued out of its instincts by adult sophistry. What had become of her passive personality?

"You are now the owner of two and a half million dollars—that is about five hundred thousand pounds. Five—hundred thousand—pounds. Think of ten sovereigns—ten golden sovereigns like that Mrs. Leadbatter gave you. Then ten times as much as that, and ten times as much as all that"—he spread his arms wider and wider—"and ten times as much as all that, and then"—here his arms were prematurely horizontal, so he concluded hastily but impressively—"and then FIFTY times as much as all that. Do you understand how rich you are?"

"Yessir." She was fumbling nervously at her gloves, half drawing them off.

"Now all this money will last for ever. For you invest it—if only at three per cent.—never mind what that is—and then you get fifteen thousand a year—fifteen thousand golden sovereigns to spend every—"

"Please, sir, I must go now. Rosie!"

"Oh, but you can't go yet. I have lots more to tell you."

"Yessir; but can't you ring for me again?"

In the gravity of the crisis, the remark tickled him; he laughed with a strange ring in his laughter.

"All right; run away, you sly little puss."

He smiled on as he poured out his tea; finding a relief in prolonging his sense of the humour of the suggestion, but his heart was heavy, and his brain a whirl. He did not ring again till he had finished tea.

She came in, and took her gloves out of her pocket.

"No! no!" he cried, strangely exasperated: "An end to this farce! Put them away. You don't need gloves any more."

She squeezed them into her pocket nervously, and began to clear away the things, with abrupt movements, looking askance every now and then at the overcast handsome face.

At last he nerved himself to the task and said: "Well, as I was saying, Mary Ann, the first thing for you to think of is to make sure of all this money—this fifteen thousand pounds a year. You see you will be able to live in a fine manor house—such as the squire lived in in your village—surrounded by a lovely park with a lake in it for swans and boats—"

Mary Ann had paused in her work, slop-basin in hand. The concrete details were beginning to take hold of her imagination.

"Oh, but I should like a farm better," she said. "A large farm with great pastures and ever so many cows and pigs and outhouses, and a—oh, just like Atkinson's farm. And meat every day, with pudding on Sundays! Oh, if father was alive, wouldn't he be glad!"

"Yes, you can have a farm—anything you like."

"Oh, how lovely! A piano?"

"Yes—six pianos."

"And you will learn me?"

He shuddered and hesitated.

"Well—I can't say, Mary Ann."

"Why not? Why won't you? You said you would! You learn Rosie."

"I may not be there, you see," he said, trying to put a spice of playfulness into his tones.

"Oh, but you will," she said feverishly. "You will take me there. We will go there instead of where you said—instead of the green waters." Her eyes were wild and witching.

He groaned inwardly.

"I cannot promise you now," he said slowly. "Don't you see that everything is altered?"

"What's altered? You are here, and here am I." Her apprehension made her almost epigrammatic.

"Ah, but you are quite different now, Mary Ann."

"I'm not—I want to be with you just the same."

He shook his head. "I can't take you with me," he said decisively.

"Why not?" She caught hold of his arm entreatingly.

"You are not the same Mary Ann—to other people. You are a somebody. Before you were a nobody. Nobody cared or bothered about you—you were no more than a dead leaf whirling in the street."

"Yes, you cared and bothered about me," she cried, clinging to him.

Her gratitude cut him like a knife. "The eyes of the world are on you now," he said. "People will talk about you if you go away with me now."

"Why will they talk about me? What harm shall I do them?"

Her phrases puzzled him.

"I don't know that you will harm them," he said slowly, "but you will harm yourself."

"How will I harm myself?" she persisted.

"Well, one day you will want a—a husband. With all that money it is only right and proper you should marry—"

"No, Mr. Lancelot, I don't want a husband. I don't want to marry. I should never want to go away from you."

There was another painful silence. He sought refuge in a brusque playfulness.

"I see you understand I'm not going to marry you."

"Yessir."

He felt a slight relief.

"Well, then," he said, more playfully still, "suppose I wanted to go away from you, Mary Ann?"

"But you love me," she said, unaffrighted.

He started back perceptibly.

After a moment, he replied, still playfully, "I never said so."

"No, sir; but—but—"—she lowered her eyes; a coquette could not have done it more artlessly—"but I—know it."

The accusation of loving her set all his suppressed repugnances and prejudices bristling in contradiction. He cursed the weakness that had got him into this soul-racking situation. The silence clamoured for him to speak—to do something.

"What—what were you crying about before?" he said abruptly.

"I—I don't know, sir," she faltered.

"Was it Tom's death?"

"No, sir, not much. I did think of him blackberrying with me and our little Sally—but then he was so wicked! It must have been what missus said; and I was frightened because the vicar was coming to take me away—away from you; and then—oh, I don't know—I felt—I couldn't tell you—I felt I must cry and cry, like that night when—" She paused suddenly and looked away.

"When—" he said encouragingly.

"I must go—Rosie," she murmured, and took up the tea-tray.

"That night when—" he repeated tenaciously.

"When you first kissed me," she said.

He blushed. "That—that made you cry!" he stammered. "Why?"

"Please, sir, I don't know."

"Mary Ann," he said gravely, "don't you see that when I did that I was—like your brother Tom?"

"No, sir. Tom didn't kiss me like that."

"I don't mean that, Mary Ann; I mean I was wicked."

Mary Ann stared at him.

"Don't you think so, Mary Ann?"

"Oh no, sir. You were very good."

"No, no, Mary Ann. Don't say good."

"Ever since then I have been so happy," she persisted.

"Oh, that was because you were wicked, too," he explained grimly. "We have both been very wicked, Mary Ann; and so we had better part now, before we get more wicked."

She stared at him plaintively, suspecting a lurking irony, but not sure.

"But you didn't mind being wicked before!" she protested.

"I'm not so sure I mind now. It's for your sake, Mary Ann, believe me, my dear." He took her bare hand kindly, and felt it burning. "You're a very simple, foolish little thing—yes, you are. Don't cry. There's no harm in being simple. Why, you told me yourself how silly you were once when you brought your dying mother cakes and flowers to take to your dead little sister. Well, you're just as foolish and childish now, Mary Ann, though you don't know it any more than you did then. After all, you're only nineteen. I found it out from the vicar's letter. But a time will come—yes, I'll warrant in only a few months' time you'll see how wise I am and how sensible you have been to be guided by me. I never wished you any harm, Mary

Ann, believe me, my dear, I never did. And I hope, I do hope so much that this money will make you happy. So, you see, you mustn't go away with me now. You don't want everybody to talk of you as they did of your brother Tom, do you, dear? Think what the vicar would say."

But Mary Ann had broken down under the touch of his hand and the gentleness of his tones.

"I was a dead leaf so long, I don't care!" she sobbed passionately. "Nobody never bothered to call me wicked then. Why should I bother now?"

Beneath the mingled emotions her words caused him was a sense of surprise at her recollection of his metaphor.

"Hush! You're a silly little child," he repeated sternly. "Hush! or Mrs. Leadbatter will hear you." He went to the door and closed it tightly. "Listen, Mary Ann! Let me tell you once for all, that even if you were fool enough to be willing to go with me, I wouldn't take you with me. It would be doing you a terrible wrong."

She interrupted him quietly,

"Why more now than before?"

He dropped her hand as if stung, and turned away. He knew he could not answer that to his own satisfaction, much less to hers.

"You're a silly little baby," he repeated resentfully. "I think you had better go down now. Missus will be wondering."

Mary Ann's sobs grew more spasmodic. "You are going away without me," she cried hysterically.

He went to the door again, as if apprehensive of an eavesdropper. The scene was becoming terrible. The passive personality had developed with a vengeance.

"Hush, hush!" he cried imperatively.

"You are going away without me. I shall never see you again."

"Be sensible, Mary Ann. You will be—"

"You won't take me with you."

"How can I take you with me?" he cried brutally, losing every vestige of tenderness for this distressful vixen. "Don't you understand that it's impossible—unless I marry you?" he concluded contemptuously.

Mary Ann's sobs ceased for a moment.

"Can't you marry me, then?" she said plaintively.

"You know it is impossible," he replied curtly.

"Why is it impossible?" she breathed.

"Because—" He saw her sobs were on the point of breaking out, and had not the courage to hear them afresh. He dared not wound her further by telling her straight out that, with all her money, she was ridiculously unfit to bear his name—that it was already a condescension for him to have offered her his companionship on any terms.

He resolved to temporise again.

"Go downstairs now, there's a good girl; and I'll tell you in the morning. I'll think it over. Go to bed early and have a long, nice sleep—missus will let you—now. It isn't Monday yet; we have plenty of time to talk it over."

She looked up at him with large, appealing eyes, uncertain, but calming down.

"Do, now, there's a dear." He stroked her wet cheek soothingly.

"Yessir," and almost instinctively she put up her lips for a good-night kiss. He brushed them hastily with his. She went out softly, drying her eyes. His own grew moist—he was touched by the pathos of her implicit trust. The soft warmth of her lips still thrilled him. How sweet and loving she was! The little dialogue rang in his brain.

"Can't you marry me, then?"

"You know it is impossible."

"Why is it impossible?"

"Because—"

"Because what?" an audacious voice whispered. Why should he not? He stilled the voice, but it refused to be silent—was obdurate, insistent, like Mary Ann herself. "Because—oh, because of a hundred things," he told it. "Because she is no fit mate for me—because she would degrade me, make me ridiculous—an unfortunate fortune-hunter, the butt of the witlings. How could I take her about as my wife? How could she receive my friends? For a housekeeper—a good, loving housekeeper—she is perfection, but for a wife—my wife—the companion of my soul—impossible!"

"Why is it impossible?" repeated the voice, catching up the cue. And then, from that point, the dialogue began afresh.

"Because this, and because that, and because the other—in short, because I am Lancelot and she is merely Mary Ann."

"But she is not merely Mary Ann any longer," urged the voice.

"Yes, for all her money, she is merely Mary Ann. And am I to sell myself for her money—I who have stood out so nobly, so high-mindedly, through all these years of privation and struggle! And her money is all in dollars. Pah! I smell the oil. Struck ile! Of all things in the world, her brother should just go and strike ile!" A great shudder traversed his form. "Everything seems to have been arranged out of pure cussedness, just to spite me. She would have been happier without the money, poor child—without the money, but with me. What will she do with all her riches? She will only be wretched—like me."

"Then why not be happy together?"

"Impossible."

"Why is it impossible?"

"Because her dollars would stick in my throat—the oil would make me sick. And what would Peter say, and my brother (not that I care what he says), and my acquaintances?"

"What does that matter to you? While you were a dead leaf nobody bothered to talk about you; they let you starve—you, with your genius—now you can let them talk—you, with your heiress. Five hundred thousand pounds. More than you will make with all your operas if you live a century. Fifteen thousand a year. Why, you could have all your works performed at your own expense, and for your own sole pleasure if you chose, as the King of Bavaria listened to Wagner's operas. You could devote your life to the highest art—nay, is it not a duty you owe to the world? Would it not be a crime against the future to draggle your wings with sordid cares, to sink to lower aims by refusing this heaven-sent boon?"

The thought clung to him. He rose and laid out heaps of muddled manuscript—opera disjecta—and turned their pages.

"Yes—yes—give us life!" they seemed to cry to him. "We are dead drops of ink, wake us to life and beauty. How much longer are we to lie here, dusty in death? We have waited so patiently—have pity on us, raise us up from our silent tomb, and we will fly abroad through the whole earth, chanting your glory; yea, the world shall be filled to eternity with the echoes of our music and the splendour of your name."

But he shook his head and sighed, and put them back in their niches, and placed the comic opera he had begun in the centre of the table.

"There lie the only dollars that will ever come my way," he said aloud. And, humming the opening bars of a lively polka from the manuscript, he took up his pen and added a few notes. Then he paused; the polka would not come—the other voice was louder.

"It would be a degradation," he repeated, to silence it. "It would be merely for her money. I don't love her."

"Are you so sure of that?"

"If I really loved her I shouldn't refuse to marry her."

"Are you so sure of that?"

"What's the use of all this wire-drawing?—the whole thing is impossible."

"Why is it impossible?"

He shrugged his shoulders impatiently, refusing to be drawn back into the eddy, and completed the bar of the polka.

Then he threw down his pen, rose and paced the room in desperation.

"Was ever any man in such a dilemma?" he cried aloud.

"Did ever any man get such a chance?" retorted his silent tormentor.

"Yes, but I mustn't seize the chance—it would be mean."

"It would be meaner not to. You're not thinking of that poor girl—only of yourself. To leave her now would be more cowardly than to have left her when she was merely Mary Ann. She needs you even more now that she will be surrounded by sharks and adventurers. Poor, poor Mary Ann. It is you who have the right to protect her now; you were kind to her when the world forgot her. You owe it to yourself to continue to be good to her."

"No, no, I won't humbug myself. If I married her it would only be for her money."

"No, no, don't humbug yourself. You like her. You care for her very much. You are thrilling at this very moment with the remembrance of her lips to-night. Think of what life will be with her—life full of all that is sweet and fair—love and riches, and leisure for the highest art, and fame and the promise of immortality. You are irritable, sensitive, delicately organised; these sordid, carking cares, these wretched struggles, these perpetual abasements of your highest self—a few more years of them—they will wreck and ruin you, body and soul. How many men of genius have married their housekeepers even—good clumsy, homely bodies, who have kept their husbands' brain calm and his pillow smooth. And again, a man of genius is the one man who can marry anybody. The world expects him to be eccentric. And Mary Ann is no coarse city weed, but a sweet country bud. How splendid will be her blossoming under the sun! Do not fear that she will ever shame you; she will look beautiful, and men will not ask her to talk. Nor will you want her to talk. She will sit silent in the cosy room where you are working, and every now and again you will glance up from your work at her and draw inspiration from her sweet presence. So pull yourself together, man; your troubles are over, and life henceforth one long blissful dream. Come, burn me that tinkling, inglorious comic opera, and let the whole sordid past mingle with its ashes."

So strong was the impulse—so alluring the picture—that he took up the comic opera and walked towards the fire, his fingers itching to throw it in. But he sat down again after a moment and went on with his work. It was imperative he should make progress with it; he could not afford to waste his time—which was money—because another person—Mary Ann to wit—had come into a superfluity of both. In spite of which the comic opera refused to advance; somehow he did not feel in the mood for gaiety; he threw down his pen in despair and disgust. But the idea of not being able to work rankled in him. Every hour seemed suddenly precious—now that he had resolved to make money in earnest—now that for a year or two he could have no other aim or interest in life. Perhaps it was that he wished to overpower the din of contending thoughts. Then a happy thought came to him. He rummaged out Peter's ballad. He would write a song on the model of that, as Peter had recommended—something tawdry and sentimental, with a cheap accompaniment. He placed the ballad on the rest and started going through it to get himself in the vein. But to-night the air seemed to breathe an ineffable melancholy, the words—no longer mawkish—had grown infinitely pathetic:

"Kiss me, good-night, dear love,
Dream of the old delight;
My spirit is summoned above,
Kiss me, dear love, good-night!"

The hot tears ran down his cheeks, as he touched the keys softly and lingeringly. He could go no further than the refrain; he leant his elbows on the keyboard, and dropped his head upon his arms. The clashing notes jarred like a hoarse cry, then vibrated slowly away into a silence that was broken only by his sobs. He rose late the next day, after a sleep that was one prolonged nightmare, full of agonised, abortive striving after something that always eluded him, he knew not what. And when he woke—after a momentary breath of relief at the thought of the unreality of these vague horrors—he woke to the heavier nightmare of reality. Oh, those terrible dollars!

He drew the blind, and saw with a dull acquiescence that the brightness of the May had fled. The wind was high—he heard it fly past, moaning. In the watery sky, the round sun loomed silver-pale and blurred. To his fevered eye it looked like a worn dollar.

He turned away shivering, and began to dress. He opened the door a little, and pulled in his lace-up boots, which were polished in the highest style of art. But when he tried to put one on, his toes stuck fast in the opening and refused to advance. Annoyed, he put his hand in, and drew out a pair of tan gloves, perfectly new. Astonished, he inserted his hand again and drew out another pair, then another. Reddening uncomfortably, for he divined something of the meaning, he examined the left boot, and drew out three more pairs of gloves, two new and one slightly soiled.

He sank down, half dressed, on the bed with his head on his breast, leaving his boots and Mary Ann's gloves scattered about the floor. He was angry, humiliated; he felt like laughing, and he felt like sobbing.

At last he roused himself, finished dressing, and rang for breakfast. Rosie brought it up.

"Hullo! Where's Mary Ann?" he said lightly.

"She's above work now," said Rosie, with an unamiable laugh. "You know about her fortune."

"Yes; but your mother told me she insisted on going about her work till Monday."

"So she said yesterday—silly little thing! But to-day she says she'll only help mother in the kitchen—and do all the boots of a morning. She won't do any more waiting."

"Ah!" said Lancelot, crumbling his toast.

"I don't believe she knows what she wants," concluded Rosie, turning to go.

"Then I suppose she's in the kitchen now?" he said, pouring out his coffee down the side of his cup.

"No, she's gone out now, sir."

"Gone out!" He put down the coffee-pot—his saucer was full. "Gone out where?"

"Only to buy things. You know her vicar is coming to take her away the day after tomorrow, and mother wanted her to look tidy enough to travel with the vicar; so she gave her a sovereign."

"Ah yes; your mother said something about it."

"And yet she won't answer the bells," said Rosie, "and mother's asthma is worse, so I don't know whether I shall be able to take my lesson to-day, Mr. Lancelot. I'm so sorry, because it's the last."

Rosie probably did not intend the ambiguity of the phrase. There was real regret in her voice.

"Do you like learning, then?" said Lancelot, softened, for the first time, towards his pupil. His nerves seemed strangely flaccid to-day. He did not at all feel the relief he should have felt at foregoing his daily infliction.

"Ever so much, sir. I know I laugh too much, sometimes; but I don't mean it, sir. I suppose I couldn't go on with the lessons after you leave here?" She looked at him wistfully.

"Well"—he had crumbled the toast all to little pieces now—"I don't quite know. Perhaps I shan't go away after all."

Rosie's face lit up. "Oh, I'll tell mother," she exclaimed joyously.

"No, don't tell her yet; I haven't quite settled. But if I stay—of course the lessons can go on as before."

"Oh, I do hope you'll stay," said Rosie, and went out of the room with airy steps, evidently bent on disregarding his prohibition, if, indeed, it had penetrated to her consciousness.

Lancelot made no pretence of eating breakfast; he had it removed, and then fished out his comic opera. But nothing would flow from his pen; he went over to the window, and stood thoughtfully drumming on the panes with it, and gazing at the little drab-coloured street, with its high roof of mist, along which the faded dollar continued to spin imperceptibly. Suddenly he saw Mary Ann turn the corner, and come along towards the house, carrying a big parcel and a paper bag in her ungloved hands. How buoyantly she walked! He had never before seen her move in free space, nor realised how much of the grace of a sylvan childhood remained with her still. What a pretty colour there was on her cheeks, too!

He ran down to the street door and opened it before she could knock. The colour on her cheeks deepened at the sight of him, but now that she was near he saw her eyes were swollen with crying.

"Why do you go out without gloves, Mary Ann?" he inquired sternly. "Remember you're a lady now."

She started and looked down at his boots, then up at his face.

"Oh yes, I found them, Mary Ann. A nice graceful way of returning me my presents, Mary Ann. You might at least have waited till Christmas, then I should have thought Santa Claus sent them."

"Please, sir, I thought it was the surest way for me to send them back."

"But what made you send them back at all?"

Mary Ann's lip quivered, her eyes were cast down. "Oh—Mr. Lancelot—you know," she faltered.

"But I don't know,' he said sharply.

"Please let me go downstairs, Mr. Lancelot. Missus must have heard me come in."

"You shan't go downstairs till you've told me what's come over you. Come upstairs to my room."

"Yessir."

She followed him obediently. He turned round brusquely, "Here, give me your parcels." And almost snatching them from her, he carried them upstairs and deposited them on his table on top of the comic opera.

"Now, then, sit down. You can take off your hat and jacket."

"Yessir."

He helped her to do so.

"Now, Mary Ann, why did you return me those gloves?"

"Please, sir, I remember in our village when—when"—she felt a diffidence in putting the situation into words, and wound up quickly—"something told me I ought to."

"I don't understand you," he grumbled, comprehending only too well. "But why couldn't you come in and give them to me instead of behaving in that ridiculous way?"

"I didn't want to see you again," she faltered.

He saw her eyes were welling over with tears.

"You were crying again last night," he said sharply.

"Yessir."

"But what did you have to cry about now? Aren't you the luckiest girl in the world?"

"Yessir."

As she spoke a flood of sunlight poured suddenly into the room; the sun had broken through the clouds, the worn dollar had become a dazzling gold-piece. The canary stirred in its cage.

"Then what were you crying about?"

"I didn't want to be lucky."

"You silly girl—I have no patience with you. And why didn't you want to see me again?"

"Please, Mr. Lancelot, I knew you wouldn't like it."

"What ever put that into your head?"

"I knew it, sir," said Mary Ann firmly. "It came to me when I was crying. I was thinking all sorts of things—of my mother and our Sally, and the old pig that used to get so savage, and about the way the organ used to play in church, and then all at once somehow I knew it would be best for me to do what you told me—to buy my dress and go back with the vicar, and be a good girl, and not bother you, because you were so good to me, and it was wrong for me to worry you and make you miserable."

"Tw-oo! Tw-oo!" It was the canary starting on a preliminary carol.

"So I thought it best," she concluded tremulously, "not to see you again. It would only be two days, and after that it would be easier. I could always be thinking of you just the same, Mr. Lancelot, always. That wouldn't annoy you, sir, would it? Because you know, sir, you wouldn't know it."

Lancelot was struggling to find a voice. "But didn't you forget something you had to do, Mary Ann?" he said in hoarse accents.

She raised her eyes swiftly a moment, then lowered them again.

"I don't know; I didn't mean to," she said apologetically.

"Didn't you forget that I told you to come to me and get my answer to your question?"

"No, sir, I didn't forget. That was what I was thinking of all night."

"About your asking me to marry you?"

"Yessir."

"And my saying it was impossible?"

"Yessir; and I said, 'Why is it impossible?' and you said, 'Because—' and then you left off; but please, Mr. Lancelot, I didn't want to know the answer this morning."

"But I want to tell you. Why don't you want to know?"

"Because I found out for myself, Mr. Lancelot. That's what I found out when I was crying—but there was nothing to find out, sir. I knew it all along. It was silly of me to ask you—but you know I am silly sometimes, sir, like I was when my mother was dying. And that was why I made up my mind not to bother you any more, Mr. Lancelot, I knew you wouldn't like to tell me straight out."

"And what was the answer you found out? Ah, you won't speak. It looks as if you don't like to tell me straight out. Come, come, Mary Ann, tell me why—why—it is impossible."

She looked up at last and said slowly and simply, "Because I am not good enough for you, Mr. Lancelot."

He put his hands suddenly to his eyes. He did not see the flood of sunlight—he did not hear the mad jubilance of the canary.

"No, Mary Ann," his voice was low and trembling. "I will tell you why it is impossible. I didn't know last night, but I know now. It is impossible, because—you are right, I don't like to tell you straight out."

She opened her eyes wide, and stared at him in puzzled expectation.

"Mary Ann"—he bent his head—"it is impossible—because I am not good enough for you."

Mary Ann grew scarlet. Then she broke into a little nervous laugh. "Oh, Mr. Lancelot, don't make fun of me."

"Believe me, my dear," he said tenderly, raising his head, "I wouldn't make fun of you for two million million dollars. It is the truth—the bare, miserable, wretched truth. I am not worthy of you, Mary Ann."

"I don't understand you, sir," she faltered.

"Thank Heaven for that!" he said, with the old whimsical look. "If you did you would think meanly of me ever after. Yes, that is why, Mary Ann. I am a selfish brute—selfish to the last beat of my heart, to the inmost essence of my every thought. Beethoven is worth two of me, aren't you, Beethoven?" The spaniel, thinking himself called, trotted over. "He never calculates—he just comes and licks my hand— don't look at me as if I were mad, Mary Ann. You don't understand me—thank Heaven again. Come now! Does it never strike you that if I were to marry you, now, it would be only for your two and a half million dollars?"

"No, sir," faltered Mary Ann.

"I thought not," he said triumphantly. "No, you will always remain a fool, I am afraid, Mary Ann."

She met his contempt with an audacious glance.

"But I know it wouldn't be for that, Mr. Lancelot."

"No, no, of course it wouldn't be, not now. But it ought to strike you just the same. It doesn't make you less a fool, Mary Ann. There! There! I don't mean to be unkind, and, as I think I told you once before, it's not so very dreadful to be a fool. A rogue is a worse thing, Mary Ann. All I want to do is to open your eyes. Two and a half million dollars are an awful lot of money—a terrible lot of money. Do you know how long it will be before I make two million dollars, Mary Ann?"

"No, sir." She looked at him wonderingly.

"Two million years. Yes, my child, I can tell you now. You thought I was rich and grand, I know, but all the while I was nearly a beggar. Perhaps you thought I was playing the piano—yes, and teaching Rosie—for my amusement; perhaps you thought I sat up writing half the night out of—sleeplessness," he smiled at the phrase, "or a wanton desire to burn Mrs. Leadbatter's gas. No, Mary Ann, I have to get my own living by hard work—by good work if I can, by bad work if I must—but always by hard work. While you will have fifteen thousand pounds a year, I shall be glad, overjoyed, to get fifteen hundred. And while I shall be grinding away body and soul for my fifteen hundred, your fifteen thousand will drop into your pockets, even if you keep your hands there all day. Don't look so sad, Mary Ann. I'm not blaming you. It's not your fault in the least. It's only one of the many jokes of existence. The only reason I want to drive this into your head is to put you on your guard. Though I don't think myself good enough to marry you, there are lots of men who will think they are . . . though they don't know you. It is you, not me, who are grand and rich, Mary Ann . . . beware of men like me—poor and selfish. And when you do marry—"

"Oh, Mr. Lancelot!" cried Mary Ann, bursting into tears at last, "why do you talk like that? You know I shall never marry anybody else."

"Hush, hush! Mary Ann! I thought you were going to be a good girl and never cry again. Dry your eyes now, will you?"

"Yessir."

"Here, take my handkerchief."

"Yessir. . . but I won't marry anybody else."

"You make me smile, Mary Ann.
When you brought your mother that cake for
Sally you didn't know a time would come when—"

"Oh, please, sir, I know that. But you said yesterday I was a young woman now. And this is all different to that."

"No, it isn't, Mary Ann. When they've put you to school, and made you a ward in Chancery, or something, and taught you airs and graces, and dressed you up"—a pang traversed his heart, as the picture of her in the future flashed for a moment upon his inner eye—"why, by that time, you'll be a different Mary Ann, outside and inside. Don't shake your head; I know better than you. We grow and become different. Life is full of chances, and human beings are full of changes, and nothing remains fixed."

"Then, perhaps"—she flushed up, her eyes sparkled—"perhaps"—she grew dumb and sad again.

"Perhaps what?"

He waited for her thought. The rapturous trills of the canary alone possessed the silence.

"Perhaps you'll change, too." She flashed a quick deprecatory glance at him—her eyes were full of soft light.

This time he was dumb.

"Sw—eêt!" trilled the canary, "Sw—eêt!" though Lancelot felt the throbbings of his heart must be drowning its song.

"Acutely answered," he said at last. "You're not such a fool after all, Mary Ann. But I'm afraid it will never be, dear. Perhaps if I also made two million dollars, and if I felt I had grown worthy of you, I might come to you and say—two and two are four—let us go into partnership. But then, you see," he went on briskly, "the odds are I may never even have two thousand. Perhaps I'm as much a duffer in music as in other things. Perhaps you'll be the only person in the world who has ever heard my music, for no one will print it, Mary Ann. Perhaps I shall be that very common thing—a complete failure—and be worse off than even you ever were, Mary Ann."

"Oh, Mr. Lancelot, I'm so sorry." And her eyes filled again with tears.

"Oh, don't be sorry for me. I'm a man. I dare say I shall pull through. Just put me out of your mind, dear. Let all that happened at Baker's Terrace be only a bad dream—a very bad dream, I am afraid I must call it. Forget me, Mary Ann. Everything will help you to forget me, thank Heaven; it'll be the best thing for you. Promise me now."

"Yessir . . . if you will promise me."

"Promise you what?"

"To do me a favour."

"Certainly, dear, if I can."

"You have the money, Mr. Lancelot, instead of me—I don't want it, and then you could—"

"Now, now, Mary Ann," he interrupted, laughing nervously, "you're getting foolish again, after talking so sensibly."

"Oh, but why not?" she said plaintively.

"It is impossible," he said curtly.

"Why is it impossible?" she persisted.

"Because—" he began, and then he realised with a start that they had come back again to that same old mechanical series of questions—if only in form.

"Because there is only one thing I could ever bring myself to ask you for in this world," he said slowly.

"Yes; what is that?" she said flutteringly.

He laid his hand tenderly on her hair.

"Merely Mary Ann."

She leapt up: "Oh, Mr. Lancelot, take me, take me! You do love me! You do love me!"

He bit his lip. "I am a fool," he said roughly. "Forget me. I ought not to have said anything. I spoke only of what might be—in the dim future—if the—chances and changes of life bring us together again—as they never do. No! You were right, Mary Ann. It is best we should not meet again. Remember your resolution last night."

"Yessir." Her submissive formula had a smack of sullenness, but she regained her calm, swallowing the lump in her throat that made her breathing difficult.

"Good-bye, then, Mary Ann," he said, taking her hard red hands in his.

"Good-bye, Mr. Lancelot." The tears she would not shed were in her voice. "Please, sir—could you—couldn't you do me a favour?—Nothing about money, sir."

"Well, if I can," he said kindly.

"Couldn't you just play Good-night and Good-bye, for the last time? You needn't sing it—only play it."

"Why, what an odd girl you are!" he said, with a strange, spasmodic laugh. "Why, certainly! I'll do both, if it will give you any pleasure."

And, releasing her hands, he sat down to the piano, and played the introduction softly. He felt a nervous thrill going down his spine as he plunged into the mawkish words. And when he came to the refrain, he had an uneasy sense that Mary Ann was crying—he dared not look at her. He sang on bravely:

"Kiss me, good-night, dear love,
Dream of the old delight;
My spirit is summoned above,
Kiss me, dear love, good-night."

He couldn't go through another verse—he felt himself all a-quiver, every nerve shattered. He jumped up. Yes, his conjecture had been right. Mary Ann was crying. He laughed spasmodically again. The thought had occurred to him how vain Peter would be if he could know the effect of his commonplace ballad.

"There, I'll kiss you too, dear!" he said huskily, still smiling. "That'll be for the last time."

Their lips met, and then Mary Ann seemed to fade out of the room in a blur of mist.

An instant after there was a knock at the door.

"Forgot her parcels after a last good-bye," thought Lancelot, and continued to smile at the comicality of the new episode.

He cleared his throat.

"Come in," he cried, and then he saw that the parcels were gone, too, and it must be Rosie.

But it was merely Mary Ann.

"I forgot to tell you, Mr. Lancelot," she said—her accents were almost cheerful—"that I'm going to church to-morrow morning."

"To church!" he echoed.

"Yes, I haven't been since I left the village, but missus says I ought to go in case the vicar asks me what church I've been going to."

"I see," he said, smiling on.

She was closing the door when it opened again, just revealing Mary Ann's face.

"Well?" he said, amused.

"But I'll do your boots all the same, Mr. Lancelot." And the door closed with a bang.

They did not meet again. On the Monday afternoon the vicar duly came and took Mary Ann away. All Baker's Terrace was on the watch, for her story had now had time to spread. The weather remained bright. It was cold, but the sky was blue. Mary Ann had borne up wonderfully, but she burst into tears as she got into the cab.

"Sweet, sensitive little thing!" said Baker's Terrace.

"What a good woman you must be, Mrs. Leadbatter," said the vicar, wiping his spectacles.

As part of Baker's Terrace, Lancelot witnessed the departure from his window, for he had not left after all.

Beethoven was barking his short, snappy bark the whole time at the unwonted noises and the unfamiliar footsteps; he almost extinguished the canary, though that was clamorous enough.

"Shut up, you noisy little devils!" growled Lancelot. And taking the comic opera he threw it on the dull fire. The thick sheets grew slowly blacker and blacker, as if with rage; while Lancelot thrust the five five-pound notes into an envelope addressed to the popular composer, and scribbled a tiny note:

"DEAR PETER,—If you have not torn up that cheque I shall be glad of it by return.

"Yours, "LANCELOT.

"P.S.—I send by this post a Reverie, called 'Marianne,' which is the best thing I have done, and should be glad if you could induce Brahmson to look at it."

A big, sudden blaze, like a jubilant bonfire, shot up in the grate and startled Beethoven into silence.

But the canary took it for an extra flood of sunshine, and trilled and demi-semi-quavered like mad.

"Sw—eêt! Sweêt!"

"By Jove!" said Lancelot, starting up, "Mary Ann's left her canary behind!"

Then the old whimsical look came over his face.

"I must keep it for her," he murmured. "What a responsibility! I suppose I oughtn't to let Rosie look after it any more. Let me see, what did Peter say? Canary seed biscuits . . . yes, I must be careful not to give it butter. . . . Curious I didn't think of her canary when I sent back all those gloves . . . but I doubt if I could have squeezed it in—my boots are only sevens after all—to say nothing of the cage."

Israel Zangwill – A Short Biography

Israel Zangwill was born in London on 21st January 1864, to a family of Jewish immigrants from the Russian Empire. His father, Moses, was from modern-day Latvia, and his mother, Ellen Hannah Marks Zangwill, from modern-day Poland.

Zangwill was initially educated in Plymouth and Bristol. At age 9 he was enrolled into the Jews' Free School in Spitalfields in east London. The school was for the children of Jewish immigrants and added to its teaching, of both secular and religious matters, with supplies of clothing, food, and health care. Zangwill excelled here. He began to teach part-time at the school and eventually full time. Whilst teaching he also studied with the University of London and by 1884 had earned his BA with triple honours in philosophy, history, and the sciences.

He had already co-written a tale entitled 'The Premier and the Painter' when he resigned as a teacher owing to differences with the managers of the school. Zangwill now turned to journalism for his new career path, initiating Ariel, The London Puck, as well as working in various capacities for the London press.

His writing earned him the sobriquet "the Dickens of the Ghetto" primarily based on his much lauded novel 'Children of the Ghetto: A Study of a Peculiar People' in 1892 and its glimpse of the poverty-stricken life in London's Jewish quarter.

As a writer he was keen to reflect on his political and social outlooks. His simulation of Yiddish sentence structure in English aroused great interest. His mystery work, 'The Big Bow Mystery' (1892) was the first locked room mystery novel. Social satire flowed with 'The King of Schnorrers' (1894). A follow up to 'Children of the Ghetto' was 'Ghetto Tragedies' in 1894 and 'Dreamers of the Ghetto' in 1898 which included essays on famous Jews such as Baruch Spinoza, Heinrich Heine and Ferdinand Lassalle.

Zangwill was also involved with narrowly focused Jewish issues as an assimilationist, an early Zionist, and later a territorialist. In the early 1890s he had joined the Lovers of Zion movement in England. A few years later, in 1897, he took part in the "pilgrimage" of English Jews to Palestine. That same year he also joined Theodor Herzl (considered the father of modern political Zionism) in founding the World Zionist

Organization and would take part in the first seven Zionist congresses. Zangwill was much admired as an orator and spoke movingly and eloquently on the issues he was passionate on.

In 1901 he had written that "Palestine is a country without a people; the Jews are a people without a country". On Herzl's visits to London, they worked closely together. In a debate at the Article Club in November 1901 however Zangwill was still mis-using the facts: "Palestine has but a small population of Arabs and fellahin and wandering, lawless, blackmailing Bedouin tribes." And made a direct plea to "restore the country without a people to the people without a country. For we have something to give as well as to get. We can sweep away the blackmailer—be he Pasha or Bedouin—we can make the wilderness blossom as the rose, and build up in the heart of the world a civilisation that may be a mediator and interpreter between the East and the West."

In 1902, Zangwill wrote that Palestine "remains at this moment an almost uninhabited, forsaken and ruined Turkish territory". But from this point on Zangwill began to see things differently which would, in 1905, result in his breakaway from Zionism.

Zangwill quit the established philosophy of Zionism when his plan for a homeland in Uganda was rejected and instead founded his own organisation; the Jewish Territorialist Organization. Its stated goal was to create a Jewish homeland in whatever territory in the world could be found for them. At that point in time suggestions were as varied as Canada, Australia, Mesopotamia, Argentina, Uganda and Cyrenaica.

Amongst the challenges in his life he found time to write poetry. He had translated a medieval Jewish poet in 1903 and his own volume 'Blind Children' in 1908 shows his promise in this new endeavour.

In 1908, Zangwill told a London court that he had been naive when he made his 1901 speech and had since recognised that the Arab population was twice that of the United States.

Zangwill was a supporter of both feminism and pacifism, but his greatest effect was as a writer who gained a wide audience with the idea of combining ethnicities into a single, American nation. The hero of 'The Melting Pot', proclaims: "America is God's Crucible, the great Melting-Pot where all the races of Europe are melting and reforming... Germans and Frenchmen, Irishmen and Englishmen, Jews and Russians – into the Crucible with you all! God is making the American.'"

'The Melting Pot' made Zangwill's name as an admired playwright. The title itself was popularised as the phrase to use to describe American absorption of immigrants when it ran in the United States.

When the play opened in Washington D.C. on 5th October 1909, former President Theodore Roosevelt leaned over the edge of his box and shouted, "That's a great play, Mr. Zangwill, that's a great play." In a later letter in 1912 Roosevelt went further "That particular play I shall always count among the very strong and real influences upon my thought and my life."

'The Melting Pot' shone a spotlight on America's growth through the input of its new waves of immigrants. Zangwill was writing as "a Jew who no longer wanted to be a Jew. His real hope was for a world in which the entire lexicon of racial and religious difference is thrown away."

According to Ze'ev Jabotinsky, Zangwill told him in 1916 that, "If you wish to give a country to a people without a country, it is utter foolishness to allow it to be the country of two peoples. This can only cause trouble. The Jews will suffer and so will their neighbours. One of the two: a different place must be found either for the Jews or for their neighbours".

In 1917 he wrote "'Give the country without a people,' magnanimously pleaded Lord Shaftesbury, 'to the people without a country.' Alas, it was a misleading mistake. The country holds 600,000 Arabs."

With the end of World War I, and a more clearly defined idea of a Jewish settlement in Palestine, Zangwill once more returned to the Zionist effort and made efforts on behalf of the Balfour Declaration, proclaiming the right of a Jewish homeland in Palestine

In 1921 Zangwill wrote "If Lord Shaftesbury was literally inexact in describing Palestine as a country without a people, he was essentially correct, for there is no Arab people living in intimate fusion with the country, utilizing its resources and stamping it with a characteristic impress: there is at best an Arab encampment, the break-up of which would throw upon the Jews the actual manual labor of regeneration and prevent them from exploiting the fellahin, whose numbers and lower wages are moreover a considerable obstacle to the proposed immigration from Poland and other suffering centers".

Despite his advocacy on Jewish matters he would be disappointed to know that despite Israel now being established the quarrels of the Middle East continue to divide.

Israel Zangwill died on 1st August 1926 in Midhurst, West Sussex.

Israel Zangwill – A Concise Bibliography

The Bachelors' Club (1891)
The Old Maid's Club (1892)
Children of the Ghetto: A Study of a Peculiar People (1892)
Grandchildren of the Ghetto (1892)
The Big Bow Mystery (1892)
Merely Mary Ann (1893)
The King of Schnorrers (1894)
The Master (1895) (based on the life of George Wylie Hutchinson)
Without Prejudices (1896)
Dreamers of the Ghetto (1898)
Ghetto Tragedies, (1899)
"The Return to Palestine", New Liberal Review, (Dec. 1901)
Children of the Ghetto (1902)
"Providence, Palestine and the Rothschilds", The Speaker, vol. 4, no. 125 (22 February 1902)
Selected Religious Poems (1903) Translation of the Jewish Medieval Poet Solomon in Cabirol.
The Grey Wig: Stories and Novelettes (1903)
The Serio-Comic Governess (1904)
Merely Mary Ann (1904)
Ghetto Comedies, (1907)
Blind Children (1908) Poetry
The Melting Pot (1909)

Italian Fantasies (1910) Travel
Chosen Peoples, (1919)
The War For The World (1916)
The Principle of Nationalities (1917)
Chosen Peoples (1918)
Hands Off Russia: Speech by Mr. Israel Zangwill at the Albert Hall, February 8th, 1919. London: Workers'
Socialist Federation, n.d. (1919)
The Voice of Jerusalem. (1921)

Filmography

Children of the Ghetto (1915, based on the play Children of the Ghetto)
The Melting Pot (1915, based on the play The Melting Pot)
Merely Mary Ann (1916, based on the play Merely Mary Ann)
The Moment Before (1916, based on the play The Moment of Death)
Mary Ann (1918, based on the play Merely Mary Ann)
Nurse Marjorie (1920, based on the play Nurse Marjorie)
Merely Mary Ann (1920, based on the play Merely Mary Ann)
The Bachelor's Club (1921, based on the novel We Moderns)
We Moderns (1925, based on the play We Moderns)
Too Much Money (1926, based on the play Too Much Money)
Perfect Crime (1928, based on the novel The Big Bow Mystery)
Merely Mary Ann (1931, based on the play Merely Mary Ann)
The Crime Doctor (1934, based on the novel The Big Bow Mystery)
The Verdict (1946, based on the novel The Big Bow Mystery)